**Praise for the Novels and Stories of
Tod Goldberg
Finalist for the *Los Angeles Times* Book Prize**

"A keen voice, profound insight . . . devilishly entertaining."   —*Los Angeles Times*

"Goldberg's prose is deceptively smooth, like a vanilla milk shake spiked with grain alcohol."
—*Chicago Tribune*

"[A] creepy, strangely sardonic, definitely disturbing version of Middle America . . . and that, of course, is where the fun begins."   —*LA Weekly*

"Perfect . . . with all the sleaze and glamour of the old paperbacks of fifty years ago."   —*Kirkus Reviews*

"Striking and affecting. . . . Goldberg is a gifted writer, poetic and rigorous . . . a fiction tour de force . . . a haunting book."   —January Magazine

Praise for the Series

"Likably lighthearted and cool as a smart-mouthed loner . . . cheerfully insouciant." —*The New York Times*

continued . . .

The Burn Notice Series

The Giveaway
The End Game
The Fix

burn notice
The Giveaway

TOD GOLDBERG

Based on the USA Network Television Series
Created by Matt Nix

AN OBSIDIAN MYSTERY

OBSIDIAN

Published by New American Library, a division of
Penguin Group (USA) Inc., 375 Hudson Street,
New York, New York 10014, USA
Penguin Group (Canada), 90 Eglinton Avenue East, Suite 700, Toronto,
Ontario M4P 2Y3, Canada (a division of Pearson Penguin Canada Inc.)
Penguin Books Ltd., 80 Strand, London WC2R 0RL, England
Penguin Ireland, 25 St. Stephen's Green, Dublin 2,
Ireland (a division of Penguin Books Ltd.)
Penguin Group (Australia), 250 Camberwell Road, Camberwell, Victoria 3124,
Australia (a division of Pearson Australia Group Pty. Ltd.)
Penguin Books India Pvt. Ltd., 11 Community Centre, Panchsheel Park,
New Delhi - 110 017, India
Penguin Group (NZ), 67 Apollo Drive, Rosedale, North Shore 0632,
New Zealand (a division of Pearson New Zealand Ltd.)
Penguin Books (South Africa) (Pty.) Ltd., 24 Sturdee Avenue,
Rosebank, Johannesburg 2196, South Africa

Penguin Books Ltd., Registered Offices:
80 Strand, London WC2R 0RL, England

First published by Obsidian, an imprint of New American Library,
a division of Penguin Group (USA) Inc.

First Printing, July 2010
10 9 8 7 6 5 4 3 2 1

For Wendy

ACKNOWLEDGMENTS

I am, as ever, indebted to Matt Nix for letting me play with his toys, and for his advice and insight while writing this book. Thanks also to Lee Goldberg for his constant—often in the middle of the night—support and for knowing all too well the obstacles I occasionally face. And I am ever grateful to my agent, Jennie Dunham, for always knowing the right things to say, my editors, Kristen Weber and Sandy Harding, for believing in my work and, finally, the wonderful fans of *Burn Notice*, who have made me feel a welcome part of their community.

During the course of writing these books, I use several sources as despite all appearances, I am not, in fact, a superspy. The following books were especially helpful: *Combat Leader's Field Guide* by Sgt. Maj. Brett Stoneberger and *The Little Book of Forensics* by David Owen. Also, as ever, please do not attempt to blow anything up or spy on someone based upon what you've read here.

I

When you're a spy, conducting business inside a restaurant or bar isn't just about finding a comfortable place to have a conversation; it can also save your life. You want to make sure you get out of a meeting without a bullet to the back of the head? Schedule your meeting inside a McDonald's Playland. There's no rule that says homicidal maniacs won't kill you in front of Ronald McDonald and Grimace, but the typical murderer tends to avoid crowded venues filled with small children eating Happy Meals. You want to kill someone and get away with it, do it in the middle of the night, in the person's home, and use a silencer on your gun and a pillow on the person's head, which will help absorb the sonic boom the bullet makes while traveling through the air. Do it right and you'll have enough time to wipe down all the surfaces you might have touched. Do it wrong and you can still be in a country without extradition before anyone finds the body.

In general, however, the best way to avoid getting killed or finding yourself in the position to kill someone is to live your life cleanly, pay your taxes, go on sensible vacations and then retire with a nest egg that will let you peter out in the fashion you've grown accustomed. That way you'll be able to eat or drink anywhere you desire without first making sure you know all the possible exit points, which is precisely what I did when I walked into the Purdy Lounge.

The Purdy is a perpetually dark bar in South Beach that's decorated like a 1970s living room. Specifically, a bachelor's living room. Lots of sofas, recliners, lava lamps and sticky surfaces. They even had a table stacked with board games. I was there to meet Barry, my favorite money launderer. He had called the night before and asked if I could help him out with a favor. I had the sense he wasn't looking for someone to pick him up at the airport.

After my eyes adjusted to the darkness and I figured out that the only obvious way out was the way in, I found Barry sitting across the bar in a ripped-up Barcalounger. He had something on his lap that glowed bright yellow, then red, then blue, then green and then repeated the sequence again, this time faster. When I was a little closer, I realized it was a game of some kind, which was a relief. I half expected Barry's favor was going to involve me clipping either the blue or the black wire on this device, thus saving or killing us both.

Across from Barry was an orange butterfly chair and a brown beanbag. Neither looked comfortable. Not in 1976. Not now. So I just stood in front of Barry

and hoped he'd get the hint. Or he'd stand up and
we'd walk down to the Carlito, which at least allowed
sunlight.

"When I was a kid, this game was like alien technology," Barry said.

"What was it called again?" I said. "Lite-Brite?"

He flipped it over so I could see the name in the center of the game. "Simon," Barry said. He set it back on
his lap and watched the blinking lights with great in-
tensity and then tried to match the pattern by pressing
on the corresponding lights, but kept getting it wrong.
"Like Hal."

"Like Simple Simon," I said.

"That sounds right," he said. He tried to match the
pattern again, but was met with only a blunt buzzing
sound.

"Maybe it would be easier if you took your sunglasses off," I said.

"See, that's the challenge," Barry said. "They're tinted
green. You know, to keep the harmful UVs away? So
that evens the playing field. All the colors are the same
now, just in different shades."

"That's fascinating, Barry," I said.

"Keeps the mind sharp," he said. "You want a turn
when I'm done?"

"I'll pass."

I looked around the bar. The bartender was a
college-aged girl with tattoos on her shoulder and
neck. Not like a criminal per se, but like a woman who

saw too many movies about women who work in bars or just listened to too much Lucinda Williams. One day she'd be seventy and walking these same streets with a portrait tattoo of Jimi Hendrix on her shoulder and would have to explain to her grandchild why she had a picture of a man from history on her skin. There were two men I pegged as German tourists—yellow socks, sandals, shorts with too many pockets—sitting on a sofa drinking tall glasses of beer and talking too loudly about how drunk they were while simultaneously setting their coasters on fire. There was a woman sitting alone at a table near where the DJ was setting up his rig at the other end of the lounge. She had the kind of face that made you think she might be famous or at least bought a lot of magazines with famous women on the cover. The difference was that she was sort of crying in a weird, huffing way, like she wanted everyone to know something was wrong with her, but didn't really want anyone to talk to her.

The end sum was that it didn't look like anyone here was planning on shooting me, so when Barry didn't seem to take the hint and continued to let me stand and watch him play Simon, I pulled up the beanbag and sat down. Barry gave the game one more pass and then dropped it down on the TV tray erected next to the Barcalounger. I made a mental note to never allow my mother into the Purdy, lest she decide to turn her house into a hipster dive.

"You want a drink?" Barry asked. He seemed uncomfortable, which didn't exactly make me excited. I like my felons to be comfortable. Maybe it was just that no one looks exactly in-the-moment sitting in a recliner.

"I try not to drink before 1982," I said.

Barry waved the bartender over, which caused the girl with the tats to exhale audibly, throw down the white towel she was using to absently wipe down the counter and make the long—maybe ten feet total—walk over to us in more time than I thought was humanly possible.

Barry shook his glass. "Another cranberry and vodka for me," he said, "and whatever our man Flint wants."

"I'm fine," I said to the girl.

She stared at me for a long time without saying anything and then said, "You a cop?" like I'd stumbled into an SLA meeting and now I was in big trouble. Maybe later I'd break up a clandestine conclave of the Weathermen, too.

"No," I said. "A spy." I decided not to give her the complete rundown of how I went from being a top covert operative to being a man on the run in the space of a phone call one fine afternoon in Nigeria. Besides, the words "burned spy" don't just roll off the tongue.

"I've seen you before," she said. "Another club I worked in, maybe."

"No," I said. "You're thinking of someone else. People think I look like other people all the time."

"You look like a cop," she said.

"I'm sitting in a beanbag chair," I said. "How can I look like *anything* in a beanbag chair?"

"Cops make people nervous," she said, "so don't stay long. People have a good time here. Too many cops is bad for business. People don't like to drink around 5-0."

5-0. It always amazed me how people co-opted slang from music, which, in this case, had co-opted a phrase from television. In all of Miami, there were never two people having an original thought at the same time.

"If I were you," I said, "I'd be more concerned about those guys over there in the yellow socks. I think they're KGB." The girl walked away, though this time she made it back to the bar in an appropriate amount of time.

I had to get out of Miami. When someone you don't know recognizes you, that's a bad sign. Problem was, since receiving my burn notice, I've been confined to Miami, which would be well and good if now other people weren't coming to visit me here, too. People with guns. People who wanted me dead. People who were pleased that I'd been burned and no longer had any government (or quasi shadow government) watching my back. All I had for sure anymore were my friends Sam Axe and Fiona Glenanne. Sam is a former Navy SEAL who now helps me out on the few odd jobs I take to make ends meet and Fiona is my ex-girlfriend. Or, well, she used to be my ex-girlfriend. Now she's . . . complicated. She also used to rob banks for the IRA, and periodically deals guns just for shoe money, and sometimes she helps me out with my clients, and sometimes, well, sometimes she's not my ex-girlfriend for the night, too.

Like I said: She's complicated.

And then, of course, I also had friends like Barry. People who could get me things I needed. People who referred work in my direction. People who, on a few occasions, had put their ass on the line for me. When I returned to Miami after getting my burn notice, I knew I could still turn to Barry for help. He might ask a few questions just to make sure he wasn't going to find himself looking down the barrel of a gun or staring at an indictment, but for the most part he was as cool as the other side of the pillow: He did his job, got his fee and walked away like nothing ever happened. You treated Bad Check Barry well; Bad Check Barry treated you well.

The bartender filled Barry's drink and brought it back, this time not bothering to say anything to me at first, but still staring at me with a confused look on her face. "I realize where I know you from," she said.

"*American Idol?*"

"You have a brother?"

"Depends," I said. "He owe you money?" My younger brother, Nate, has a habit of owing people money. Particularly people in bars.

"Yeah," she said. "He walked out of here without paying his tab one night last week, but the moron left his wallet on the bar. He had a picture of you in it. I only remember because I thought you were cute and wondered how such a fuckup could have such a cute brother. One of those weird things you think about on a dead night, you know? If you want, it might still be in the lost and found."

"Keep it," I said.

The girl shrugged. "Suit yourself," she said.

Barry watched her walk away. "I've been coming here for ten years, no one says a word to me. You're here ten minutes, you're already cute."

Ten minutes was already too long. "You wanted to talk to me about something, Barry?"

Barry took a sip of his drink. "I don't normally drink cranberry juice," he said, "but I'm trying to cleanse my system. Start taking a little bit better care of myself, you know? Investing in me."

"Vodka integral to that plan?"

"That's just to mask the taste of the cranberry," he said. "One-part question: How do you feel, generally, about criminals?"

"Generally? I don't care for them, Barry. Specifically, I like you. I have feelings for Fiona. Why?"

"I have a friend," he said. "He used to work in transactions."

"Transactions?"

"Banking." Barry took another sip of his drink and this time grimaced. "My mom? She used to drink cranberry juice all the time. Can't figure out why."

"Plumbing," I said.

Barry thought about that for a moment. "You know what you never see kids drinking anymore?" he asked.

"I don't spend a lot of time around children, Barry."

"Ovaltine."

"That's a tremendous insight."

"Another one? Delaware Punch. Sanka, too. No one drinks Sanka. My mom practically lived on Sanka. Sanka and cranberry juice. You think it's related?"

"I think I want you to stop avoiding whatever it is you wanted to ask me about your friend the banker," I said.

"He isn't exactly a banker," Barry said.

"Stunned," I said.

"He actually robbed banks."

"With a gun or with hundreds of bad mortgages?"

"Funny thing," Barry said, "he was known for not using a gun."

"Just charmed people into giving him their money?"

"He actually robbed safe-deposit boxes," Barry said. "That was his thing. Or it was until he got caught."

"I'm not busting your friend out of prison, Barry."

"He's out. Did a full bid at Glades, got out after twelve years for good behavior. You know they got cable in prison now?"

"I've never been to prison," I said.

"But you know such places exist?"

I checked my watch. This was now fifteen minutes I'd never get back. Across the way, the Germans were now trying to set fire to the pools of spilled beer on their table. "Barry, I don't mean any offense here. We're friends. You've done me a lot of favors. But if you don't tell me what you need in five minutes, I'm going to ask those German tourists to set me on fire."

Barry nodded once but then didn't say anything for a moment, which I took to be a bad sign. Barry isn't an especially chatty guy. Oh, he'll go on at some length about things he's really interested in—forgeries, gold bullion, places one can purchase black-market kidneys on the cheap—but what makes Barry an especially good financial criminal is that he's quick to get in and out of a situation.

"Hypothetically," Barry said, "say you found your-self stuck in a place with no way of really earning a living."

"Hypothetically."

"And you had a mother that was driving you crazy, but you loved her, and didn't want her to suffer, so when she got sick and you couldn't afford her bills, you did the one thing you've been trained to do just to keep up with your mom's prescriptions and medical appointments."

"Have you been watching me, Barry?"

"Even Charles Manson had a mom," Barry said. "And besides, this is all hypothetical. Your mother is sick, lots of bills, you have a skill set that allows you to pay those bills off with a minimum of exertion, hypo-thetically, don't you do that? I mean, for your mom?"

Thinking of all the things I'd done for my mother, Madeline, was like sticking pins in my eyes. I nearly died cleaning out the calcified remains of Tater Tots beneath the seat of her car just a few weeks previous. "Hypothetically, what did this friend of yours end up doing?"

"He might have robbed a stash house out in the Everglades."

"Either he did or he didn't."

"I thought we were still pretending this person didn't really exist?"

I pointed at my watch. "Two minutes," I said.

"Then he did."

"And how is this now my problem?"

Barry exhaled. "See, here's the thing, Michael. I like to think that you and me, we have a nice working relationship, right? You scratch my back, I scratch your back, and in the end, we both feel good, right? Just two guys who like to scratch each other, metaphorically speaking."

"Tick, tick, tick," I said.

"Now, a homeless person, a person with no real friends, whoever scratches a homeless person's back, you know? You have an itch, you have to rub yourself against a wall or something, right? You following me?"

"Not in the least, Barry, but please continue. I have to know where this ends up."

"My friend—we'll call him Bruce—he's been on

his own for a long time and now he needs someone to scratch his back, but maybe I don't have long enough arms. Or maybe I just don't know how he likes to be scratched."

"Barry," I said, "speak English."

"He wants to give what he stole back."

"Really."

"Most everything."

Most everything. Two words that might equal the entire sum of human knowledge, but probably included drugs and guns. Maybe it just meant baseball cards and Three Dog Night eight-tracks, but probably not.

"And this is from his warm core of altruism?"

"There might be some extenuating circumstances, but that's the rub on the deal. I thought maybe you could help him out. Stand behind him. Look menacing. Maybe send Fiona to lay a little ground fire. Whatever it takes."

"This Bruce," I said, "he have a last name?"

"Grossman."

I wrote his name down on a napkin. "Let me have Sam check him out. He turns out to be a fraud, he can play Robin Hood all by himself."

"I don't think Robin Hood stole from people and then gave them their stuff back," Barry said. "You're thinking of *The Thomas Crowne Affair*. The one with that guy who was James Bond."

"You get the point," I said.

"Know what I don't understand?" Barry said. "All

these guys you see in movies, running around playing spies, how come no one ever kills them? Forty years James Bond has been running around killing people and no one bothers to just drop a bomb on him? He even went to the moon. Crazy, right?"

I stood up to leave, but Barry kept his seat. "This Bruce, he a good friend?"

"Taught me a lot of my tricks," Barry said. "Back in the day, he was one of the best. An honor to the profession."

"His mom really sick or is that just a story you told to get me interested?"

"I would have used a missing or dying kid. I don't know how you feel about old ladies, but I know you got a soft spot for sick kids."

"How do you know that?"

"Everyone knows that. Got a kid with cancer and you owe fifty large to the Mafia, Michael Westen can help you."

I thought about that. It would have been a much easier way in. Helping a needy bank robber wasn't exactly my wheelhouse. "Let me check this Bruce Grossman out," I said. "I have questions, I'll find you."

"You always do," Barry said.

2

Getting information on a person who has spent the last decade behind bars is not as easy as you would think. Department of Corrections records are pretty simple affairs—they give you details on the crimes, the sentencing and any other detainers the incarcerated might have. But if you want to know if the person was a confidential informant (also known, affectionately, as a snitch), or taught the Bible study class, or routinely beat the crap out of other prisoners or was your garden-variety prison predator, you need to know someone on the inside.

Alternately, it might help if you knew someone in the FBI, if the person you were looking into happened to be one of the most successful bank robbers ever. Fortunately, Sam knew a lot of people in the FBI.

"You know what I had to do to get this information?" Sam asked. It was the next day and we were sitting on the patio of the Carlito having lunch. I was eating mine. Sam was drinking his. There was a manila file folder between us that was thick with documents.

I didn't bother to open it as Sam's favorite part of the day was always show-and-tell.

"Nothing you haven't done before," I said.

"Let me ask you something, Mikey," Sam said. "You ever feel shame for anything?"

"Not a lot, no," I said. The truth was that, of course, I felt shame for small things in my life. It's the small things that tend to bother you. Things you wish you hadn't said. People you wish you hadn't hurt. Governments you wish you hadn't helped topple. "But I'm human, Sam."

"See, that's the thing," Sam said. He opened up the folder and pulled out a picture of the inside of a safe-deposit vault in a bank. All of the drawers were pulled out. "I look at this picture and I think, man, now that's pretty impressive. Goes in. Doesn't bother grabbing dye packs. Doesn't stick a gun in anyone's face. Just pops the boxes and gets out with untraceable loot. I feel some shame in that admission. I mean, if the world were different and I hadn't pledged allegiance to peace and justice and the American Way."

"And here I thought you were talking about what you had to do to get the information," I said.

"I don't feel shame about that," Sam said. "Just sore."

"More than I need to know," I said.

Sam looked off for a moment and I got the sense that he was trying to draw me into his sense of whimsy, or debauchery, or whatever it was he was trying to convey by looking off into the distance like a person in a perfume ad. Sam has many "friends" who are able to get him information by virtue of his long standing in various overt and covert positions. Some of them just dole it out because of the kindness in their hearts. Some do it because Sam gives them something. And some do it because, apparently, Sam has certain superhuman skills best left undiscovered by those who are unwilling to hear a play-by-play, which would include me.

"You ever heard of the Flying Lotus?" Sam asked.

"Is that a restaurant?"

"Oh, no, my friend. It is not something you pay for," Sam said.

I picked up the photo Sam had been looking at and hoped that would end the portion of the conversation that Sam seemed intent on explaining. The picture showed a Crocker Bank in Walnut Creek, California. The date stamp was March 23, 1983. Over twenty-five years ago. That didn't seem right.

"How old is Grossman?" I asked.

"Sixty-five," Sam said.

"A sixty-five-year-old man robbed someone's stash house? How'd he get out alive?"

"Bruce Grossman could break into a prison and steal the bars," Sam said. "The guy is a legend."

Sam handed me a stack of photos. Bank of America in Deer Park, Washington. Wells Fargo in Chicago. Lincoln Savings in Tonopah, Arizona. Citibank in Miami.

University credit unions in about thirty different small towns across the middle of the country. And this was just the 1980s. All safe-deposit boxes. The last photo he showed me was Grossman's booking photo. He looked like an accountant: Trim black hair, no facial hair, woolly eyebrows, a funny smirk on his face.

"What's he smiling about here?" I asked.

"Probably just surprised he finally got caught," Sam said.

The photos of the vaults all had one thing in common: Apart from the missing items in the boxes, the vaults looked otherwise untouched. No blast marks. No broken doors. No blood or bodies or crazy writing scrawled on the walls declaring a death to capitalist pigs. Nothing. "How'd he get in?"

"They think he rented a safe-deposit box, disabled the cameras and went to town. They also think sometimes he worked at the bank. There's some thought he worked for a janitorial service. And some people think he'd spend the night in the air ducts. Sometimes, it looks like the *Starship Enterprise* beamed him in. All of this is supposition. Guy never admitted anything. They assume these are all his jobs, but he only got nicked for the last one he did."

One thing bank robbers and spies have in common is that you're only as good as your last job. There's a reason you don't hear much about old bank robbers or old spies: Botch the job and there's usually someone with a gun waiting for you.

"He ever hurt anyone?"

"No," he said. "Way he got caught? Technology crept up on him. Years and years he'd been busting into these old branch offices, or banks in small towns, tiny credit unions, that sort of thing. In 1997 they found him inside the safe-deposit vault of that old Seminole Savings and Loan out in Doral. He got in through the roof but broke his leg on the way down. The bank had just installed laser-lock doors on the vault and that was it. Boy was stuck."

"And they weren't able to put these other jobs on him?"

"Nope," Sam said. "Never even left a fingerprint. They only tried him on the Doral job."

Sam handed me the rest of the file and I spent a few minutes reading through the documents. "Says here the FBI tried to bring him on to help their bank robbery unit," I said.

"He would have walked after six months," Sam said. "Did his whole bid instead."

"Twelve years is a long time," I said. "Glades isn't exactly Club Fed."

"Maybe he's one of those guys who believes in rehabilitation."

"Maybe he's one of those guys who believes it's safer on the inside," I said. "He stole a lot of stuff from people if these photos are to be believed. Have to think there are some people who'd like to see him dead."

"That's the crazy thing," Sam said. "He found things

he thought had some significant sentimental value for someone? He'd mail it back to the bank with a note of apology."

I shook my head. "That doesn't make any sense. Why would he do that?"

"Why do you eat yogurt?"

"I like the way it tastes."

"Maybe he liked apologizing."

My cell phone rang. It was my mother, Madeline. Just like always. I hit the MUTE button. Sam's phone rang twenty seconds later. He looked at it and hit MUTE, too.

"You give my mom all of your phone numbers now, too?"

"Mikey, she can be very persuasive."

Since returning to Miami, my mother, Madeline, has inserted herself into all of my deepest—and most mundane—relationships. It's as if all the attention she didn't give me or Nate as kids she's trying to make up for now, which is a nice sentiment, if not a completely exciting thing to actually live with. "Attention" for my mother often means me coming to her house and repairing the toaster oven or the top-loading VCR.

Anyway, my mother's call reminded me of something important. "Anything on his sick mother?"

Sam reached into his pocket and pulled out a scrap of paper that had his scribbles on it. "Bruce's release address is registered to Zadie Grossman, age eighty-eight. I'm going to guess that's not his hot young wife."

He handed me the paper. It was an address in Aventura, a section of North Miami known for its extensive Jewish community, notably a large senior citizen population. Not exactly the kind of locale one wants to find themselves in after doing more than a decade of hard time, but then maybe he missed his mother's cooking.

Still, there was something interesting about this. I owed Barry a favor or two hundred, but I had to think that a sixty-five-year-old man, ex-felon or not, living with his mother meant something.

If you really want to know about somebody, meet them when they are around their parents. When you're a spy, this isn't something that happens very often. You walk into the Libyan Embassy in Qatar and ask for Salim and Salim's mommy, the odds are you're not going to get either of them. But follow Salim for a few weeks and you'll see how often he eats at his mother's house, how often he complains to his wife that she doesn't make Sharba Libiya as well as his mother does, how often he calls his mother to just check in, make sure everything is okay, and how little regard he gives to his wife's welfare, you know you've got someone you can manipulate.

Or at least someone who isn't going to stray too far, lest his mommy needs him.

I needed to get out of Miami.

I flipped through the file and came up with several photos of a house. The address matched the one Sam gave me.

"Why is the FBI still watching him?" I asked.

"The FBI doesn't watch people, Michael, you know that." Sam reached across the table and took the file from me and fished around for a few moments and then pulled out a photo of an older gentleman wearing a red V-neck sweater, tan pants and red loafers. He carried a black satchel in his hands. "This is what Mr. Grossman looks like now."

"Looks like time did him," I said. There were lines around his eyes that brought to mind the inside of trees. The weird thing was that he was missing most of the pinkie on his right hand. "What happened to his hand?"

"Belt-sanding accident inside," Sam said.

"What kind of accident?"

"Someone tried to take off his face with a belt sander, got his finger instead."

"They keep him separate from the population after that?"

"Doesn't seem like it. Records show he was in general population the whole time," Sam said. "So, doesn't look like he snitched."

"There goes your rehabilitation angle," I said, though the truth is that if you're in prison, it's probably better for your long-term mortality to not snitch.

"Hey, maybe he had a revelation upon release," Sam said. He had a point, though not much of one. "Any guesses on what's in that satchel?"

"Girl Scout cookies," I said.

"Guess again."

"A chisel and hammer."

"One more," he said.

"Why don't you just tell me?"

"You're not fun to play games with," Sam said. "Anyway"—he was excited now, which was obvious since he stopped drinking the multiple beers he'd been nursing since we sat down and was now just toying with a knife—"that satchel contains the current membership list of the Ghouls Motorcycle Club. Your friend Mr. Grossman is in the process of surreptitiously dropping it off in front of the FBI field office on Northwest Second."

"Why would he have . . ." I began, but then stopped. "They're not watching him, are they? They're protecting him."

"Not quite," Sam said. "They're just curious how an ex-con living with his mommy happened to run across this information and then felt compelled to drop it on their doorstep. Especially since he could have just as easily dropped it with some members of the Banshees and solved a lot of problems."

The Ghouls and the Banshees were the biker gang equivalent of a family feud gone wrong. The Banshees splintered from the Ghouls a decade ago, and the resulting war between the two groups was one of those organized-crime wars that the authorities were usually happy to let happen; as long as they just killed one another, there was a net gain for society.

"He had to know there were cameras," I said, which

made me realize: *He had to know there were cameras.* And there it was. The extenuating circumstance Barry mentioned. The stash house belonged to the Ghouls Motorcycle Club, an outlaw gang whose propensity for violent crime made even the Hells Angels seem like an esteemed group of kind and generous fellows with a shared interest in motorcycles. If he was dropping off their materials at the FBI office in broad daylight, and in a bright red sweater no less, that meant he was scared.

I came back to the photos of the house in Aventura. From the outside it looked like a standing set from *Miami Vice*: the facade was faux Art Deco and statues of pink flamingos dotted the lawn. In the driveway, however, was a yellow Ford Fairmont station wagon, replete with wood paneling and a luggage rack.

"How sick is the mother?" I asked.

"Gets radiation five days a week," Sam said. "Maxed credit cards. Looks like Medicare is picking up some of the rudimentary stuff, but I guess cancer isn't all that rudimentary."

I thought about my mother, who smoked like Chernobyl but miraculously didn't have cancer. Meeting Bruce's mother might be a nice object lesson. Or it might just give her someone to smoke with. "Is she dying?"

"Old people die," Sam said. "Old people with cancer don't have improved odds, they just die more painfully."

"Let me ask you something," I said. "Why should I take this job?"

"All the people you've ever helped, you think he's half as bad as most?"

"He's a bank robber," I said.

"So is Fiona," Sam said. "And for a terrorist organization, I might add."

"That's not been substantiated," I said. "There's some muddy area concerning whether or not she knew she was working for the IRA."

"She also sells guns to criminals," Sam said. "As in she had me watch her back yesterday while you were meeting with Barry. Sold a trunkful of Russian GSh-18 pistols to some Cubans."

"Cubans?"

"Planning a revolution or something. Real beauties. Anyway, I admit that when Fiona does a little crime, it's hot, real hot, but you can't pick and choose your bad guys. Plus, while Fiona probably wouldn't smother her dying mother, she's not known for her Florence Nightingale tendencies, Mikey. At least Grossman is doing all he can to save his mother. Or at least make her comfortable."

When Sam is the voice of reason, I know there's something fundamentally wrong. But then he added, "And you owe Barry, Mikey."

Again with the voice of reason . . .

I took out my cell and called Barry.

"I'll meet with Grossman on one condition," I said.

"I take this, I need some cash, you pay my fee. I don't want whatever money he's holding on to."

"That makes me think you don't trust him," Barry said.

"I don't," I said.

"You realize I don't work nights at a Christian charity, right?"

"Your stolen money is cleaner," I said.

"That's kind."

"I also know where you live."

There was a pause on the line. "You do?" he said finally.

"Tell Grossman I'll be at his house in two hours," I said and hung up. Best to leave some questions unanswered.

3

No spy wants to work with a double agent. Even if you might want to give off the impression that you're only in the game for the money or the glory or the opportunity to visit lovely Third World nations and assassinate their leaders, even the most jaded spy probably still has a love for his country. You spend too many years training to suddenly realize you hate everyone and everything about the country you've been sworn to protect.

A double agent, however, has allegiance only to himself, and thus goes through the training because he sees a way to prosper personally. This makes trusting him nearly impossible, cornering him unrealistic. The best way to get a double agent to acquiesce to your demands, or just play nice in the sandbox, is to present him with another double agent to confuse him. Two people out for only themselves causes a certain amount of friction, particularly when there's only one of whatever they both want.

Which is why I brought Fiona with me to meet Bruce

Grossman. And why I first gave her a tour through Aventura's hottest suburban spots. There's something about suburbia that makes Fiona homicidal, and Aventura is one of those master-planned communities developed in the 1970s and 1980s to remind people what they thought the world was like in the 1950s and 1960s. Back then, the future occupants of Aventura lived in Chicago or New York or Detroit and had an idea that the suburbs would be a good place to retire to, only to find that by the time they actually retired, the suburbs were filled with the people that now scared them.

Shops and outdoor cafés dotted the streets, and every few feet there was a cluster of octogenarians in close conversation. In front of a retro-cool-looking joint called the Blintz there were two women who literally had blue hair, which would have been surprising if not for the other two making their way along Northeast 207th toward the Shoppes at the Waterways. Across the street was a cluster of high-rise condo complexes, and I imagined that at night the windows glowed blue, and not from all of the running televisions. Beside me in the Charger, Fiona made a clucking sound with her tongue, which she sometimes did when she was particularly sickened by something.

"Promise me you will shoot me if I ever do that to my hair," Fiona said.

"I promise," I said.

"Mean it," she said. "Tell me what you'd use. I want to be sure I will die."

"I'm going to guess a Russian GSh-18 would do the trick," I said.

Fiona slapped her hand against the door. "Does anyone know how to keep a secret anymore?"

"Selling arms to Cubans doesn't seem like a great idea."

"They were using them for strictly democratic aims," Fiona said. "And they paid double."

"Why didn't you ask me to cover you?"

"Because I didn't want you skulking in the background," she said. "Cubans would think you were bad juju. Sam emits good juju."

I could only shake my head. Used to be Sam and Fiona hated each other, or, at the very least, distrusted each other immensely. Now they probably pinkie-swore on their mendacity. "Fi, you don't know what could have happened."

"Michael, are you saying you were worried?"

"No," I said.

"That's very sweet," she said. She reached over and squeezed my cheek. Hard. To the point that I had to really focus with my left eye so that I didn't slam into the traffic in front of me. "I like that you were worried for me long after any danger had already passed."

"How am I supposed to know if I should be worried if you don't even tell me what you're doing?"

"You're the hero, Michael," she said. "I'm just the damsel in distress."

Sometimes I want to kiss Fiona. And sometimes I

have, and more. And then, sometimes, I wish I was in Abu Dhabi negotiating a transfer of black-market pearls into the hands of a terrorist, who would then get arrested at the airport while smuggling them into the States and I'd get to interrogate him for a nice long night.

Ah, the good times.

"I'm just saying," I said, "that I want you to be careful. People might come through you to get to me. Just be vigilant."

"Just so we're clear," she said, "this is actually about you?"

"No," I said.

Fi looked at me for a second, and I couldn't tell if she was taking all of this seriously or not. I wasn't sure if I was at first, but I was by the end. "That's terribly sweet, Michael," she said softly. And then she slapped me. "And that's for not being sweet enough to pay attention in the first place and forcing me into this weird serious conversation with you."

My face hurt. "You feel better?"

"Somewhat."

We drove in silence for a few minutes while I did jaw exercises to get my bite back in line and Fiona calmed down from her brief flirtation with actual human emotion and physical violence; her two basic states of being.

I turned down a palm tree–lined side street just off of 207th and parked in front of Zadie Grossman's house. All around the home were the long shadows of the high-rise condos, which gave the street an eerie darkness even in the middle of the day. The house also seemed anachronistic compared to the luxury we'd passed on our way here—one- and two-million-dollar homes, driveways lined with Lincolns and Cadillacs, all the plastic surgery a ninety-year-old needs in order to feel seventy—in that it just looked like a poorly decorated starter home. There were the flamingos, of course, but also a rock lawn and palm trees that looked closer to dead than paradise. It seemed oddly familiar.

And that station wagon, too.

"If he's a bank robber," Fi said, "why does his mother live in such a hideous home?"

"He's been in prison for twelve years."

"How long has he been out?"

"Six months," I said.

"That's plenty long to get a decent score. At least get rid of those flamingos. Dreadful taste."

This could have been my childhood home, I thought. I suppose I could have ended up robbing banks, too.

"And why am I here?" Fiona asked.

"To keep Bruce honest," I said. "Crook to crook."

"You might not like what you hear," she said.

"I'm prepared for that."

Fi got out of the car and I followed her up the walk, but even before we got to the door, Bruce Grossman opened it up, stepped out and closed it quietly behind him. "My mom's sleeping," he said, his voice just above a whisper.

He was tall—at least six-three—and had a body roughly the shape of a pear. His head, neck and chest were skinny, but his stomach slouched over his belt line and his legs were chubby, too. He wore a button-down blue shirt that he'd tucked into cargo shorts. On his feet were sandals and socks. He looked, essentially, like a tourist. I couldn't fathom him robbing a stash house, much less one belonging to a motorcycle gang.

Bruce reached into his back pocket and pulled out a photo and handed it to me. It was of an old woman, her hair gone, sitting poolside reading that morning's *Miami Herald*.

"What's this?" I said.

"Barry said you might want a proof-of-life photo," Bruce said. I handed it to Fiona, who looked at it for a moment, shook her head and gave it back to Bruce. "Do you want a lock of hair or something?"

"The picture is fine," I said.

Bruce looked at the photo for a second and a smile crossed his face. "When I was a kid? She had a perm. One of those tight ones, remember? Crazy, right?"

I nodded.

"And now she's bald. She always said I made her pull her hair out, but this isn't my fault," Bruce said. He laughed then, though it wasn't very funny. "Anyway, I appreciate you coming by. Do you want to see all the loot? And then, what, we just drop it off?"

"No," I said.

"No?"

"Bruce, this is my friend Fiona," I said.

"Friend?" Fiona said. She was angry. I've tried my whole life to avoid angry women. Avoiding angry Fiona should be a national pastime.

"Associate," I said.

"*Associate?*" Fiona said.

I looked at Bruce. He seemed perplexed.

"What is the right answer, Fiona?" I said.

She cocked her head at me and then ran her tongue over her teeth. I've seen nature videos where panthers do the same thing. "What is it you want me to do here?" she said. "That will determine my answer."

I took a deep breath. "Bruce, this is Fiona. She's going to interrogate you about your story, because you've clearly lied to Barry about how you came across this information you need returned. I feel like you'll probably lie to me, which will cause both of us great pain and sorrow, so I thought my . . . Fiona . . . could get the truth out of you without either of us getting hurt in the process."

Bruce got a queer look on his face. "Is she going to torture me?"

"Maybe," Fi said.

Bruce took a step back toward the door.

"No," I said. "No, she is not. No, she is absolutely not. Are you, Fiona?"

"Everyone is so dull around here," she said, a noticeable pout in her voice.

I handed my keys to Fiona. "Fiona is going to take

you for a drive, Bruce. If she likes what she hears, she'll bring you back here and we'll have a deal. If she doesn't like what she hears, she'll drive you back here and I'll be gone. Understand?"

Bruce looked over both of his shoulders and then back at both of us. We stared back at him. "I thought someone was going to come up and blindfold me. That's how the FBI does it."

"I'm not the FBI," Fiona said. She took Bruce by the hand and guided him toward the car, even opened the passenger door for him. He looked back at me, shrugged and climbed in. Fi locked him in, which gave him a visible start.

"Don't hurt him," I said.

"Not even a little?" Fi asked.

"Not even a little," I said.

Fi sighed. "One day," she said, flirtation coming back to her, "you're going to regret that I wasn't allowed to hurt more people."

She got into the car without another word, but I was pretty sure that finding out the validity of that threat would be either the best or the worst day of my life.

I watched the car round the corner at the end of the street and disappear and then made my way inside, in case Bruce's mother woke up and needed something, because even a burned spy knows how to make a glass of water.

4

The way Bruce Grossman figured it, robbing safe-deposit boxes was a victimless crime. If people kept large sums of money in safe-deposit boxes—and there were always large sums of money to be found—that meant those people were probably crooks. If you're a normal person, there's no good reason to keep your money in a place hidden from use. Oh, sure, maybe you harbor fears that the Nazis are coming or the Commies are coming or the end of the Mayan calendar is nigh and the world is coming to an end, but even still, what would having money hidden away do for you? People who hide their money do it because they are doing something wrong.

That's not to say he robbed safe-deposit boxes to get back at the bad guys, because that wasn't the case in the least. Starting out, he just wanted to have things. A nice house. A nice car. A place for his mother in a safe neighborhood in Miami. Maybe some flash cash, just so the ladies knew he was more than a receding hairline and an odd personality, because, shit, he knew he wasn't *all that*. No, starting out, that money got him places. Opened doors. Got return phone calls from smart girls.

And if he got in deep with somebody, say at the bookie's joint, he just had to pop a score in some no-name town and come back with whatever money he needed to pay off his debts. Used to be, before a night out in Detroit—back in the 1980s, that was his place to go, right in the middle of the country, easy in, easy out—he'd find a credit union near Wayne State, get what he needed and go.

But later, it was just about cost of living. He moved his mother to Miami after his father died—this was in 1992—and her bills just started piling up. At this point in his life, Bruce considered himself excellent at what he did, to the point that, in an irony even he was aware of, he had to start keeping his money in safe-deposit boxes. He even robbed a bank he had an account and safe-deposit box in, just to deflect interest, not that he thought any was coming his way. His mom, though, was in her seventies and the ailments kept compounding. So he did what any enterprising businessperson, or good son, would do: He made as much as he could and then quietly retired to Florida.

And it was a good life, at first. Bruce spent the next few years in a condo across the street from the house he bought his mother, so that way he could come over and look in on her, replace a lightbulb or two, even take her out to dinner once a week. Most nights, he drove his red Corvette convertible down to South Beach and threw money around, met a couple nice girls, even a couple guys he considered friends, guys he'd fish with, that sort of thing. And, of course, his friend Barry, whom he helped with a few start-up business ventures initially. Importing stolen items. Understanding weak points in the ceiling mortar of old buildings. Hosting pyramid schemes.

But there was something about retired life that just wasn't as exciting as robbing banks. So he'd periodically case places, you know, just to stay in shape.

And then just in case happened. His mom got her first bout of cancer, in her lungs. Doctors took out most of her left lung, a bunch of lymph nodes under her arm, stuck her in chemo for six months, radiation for another three. Thing was, she had crap for health insurance, just like everyone Bruce knew, apart from Bruce. She had Medicare, but Bruce wanted her to have good doctors, not the hacks who got government money. So out of his own pocket he flew her up to Johns Hopkins, out to LA to Cedars, even to some quack in Montreal who thought she should eat only pork and drink only lime juice.

Then, one afternoon, sitting in the waiting room at the transfusion center over in Coconut Grove, a place his mom liked to go just because it had better magazines than the chemo spot in Aventura, he got an idea while hearing two nurses bitch about their husbands.

"You know," one said—she was Cuban, so he always thought of her as Fidel—"my idiot husband, if he loses a toe, his insurance policy gives him five hundred thousand bucks. A whole foot, a million. Some nights, I think about just chopping off his big toe and getting out of town, you know?"

The other nurse, who was pretty, so Bruce just thought of her, and thought of her, and thought of her, said, "Dismemberment insurance is what keeps me sane. Bad day here, I think, cut off my pinkie, retire to the Caymans, get away from Peter forever!"

The nurses laughed and high-fived each other, but Bruce started thinking about the future, about taking care of his mom, about maybe doing something good after doing so much bad all these years.

When he got home that night, he called his insurance agent and upped his coverage, added dismemberment to the buffet, said he was doing so much fishing he was afraid he might lose something important. His agent laughed. He laughed. Even told his buddies on the boat one day. They all laughed.

And then he started plotting a way to lose a finger, maybe two, just to keep his mother in the station she'd grown accustomed to. He also thought one more good job would seal the deal.

Now, sitting in the car next to this whack job Fiona, he wasn't sure any of it was worth it. She was pretty, for sure, but he was supposed to be in business with Michael Westen, who according to Barry, was like a Jedi. He liked the idea of hiring a Jedi to help him out. Figured he could tell a few lies, leave out some

key points, what would Obi-Wan know? But then this
Fiona girl . . . she frankly scared the crap out of him,
so he just figured he'd tell the straight truth, see where
that got him. Worse came to worst, he was in the same
position as he was ten minutes ago. But she was cute,
so there was that.

"In retrospect," Bruce told Fiona, as they rounded
yet another street filled with old ladies out on their
porches talking on their portable phones or playing
solitaire, "I should have just chopped my finger off and
been done with it."

"You're enthralling me with your tale of woe," Fiona
said. "And most of it even seems plausible, except for
the part about smart girls thinking you were cute, but
what happened with the stash house?"

It was stupid, Bruce had to admit. After getting released from jail, minus a finger, minus the $500 he had
to pay to lose the finger, but plus the $750,000 his in-
surance paid out that he was able to give to his mom
for her bills while he was inside, he moved in with his
mom, determined to just be a good son, which he felt
he was. Good citizen, which meant he wouldn't help
his friend Barry do anything cash-based, just give him
some occasional advice, maybe even get a job working
at the Starbucks across the street, or the one next door,
or even the one half a block away.

And for two months it worked. Well, apart from
the Starbucks thing. He got a job instead working at
Kinko's, just to pass the time. But then his mom got

sick again—this time the cancer was in her liver—and he started thinking about giving her some comfort. She was eighty-eight now and even if it all worked out with the cancer, how much longer did she have?

The thing was, he couldn't go back to prison. And the last time he'd robbed a bank he found out the hard way that banks in Miami in the late nineties weren't like crap-ass savings and loans in small towns in Oregon: You could break into the safe-deposit boxes, you just couldn't get your ass back out, at least not with a broken leg. And that was twelve years ago. So Bruce went looking for a stash house, something run by drug dealers, so they'd be working from straight cash, and preferably crystal meth or coke dealers, since they frequently got high off of their own supply and couldn't stand to be locked up at home.

It only took him a couple of weeks of scouting, first by going to the colleges at night and watching the dealers pull up to the fraternity houses to make drops, and then later tinkering around the hot spots in South Beach, looking for actors and actresses and models with runny noses and then seeing where they went. A couple of times he thought he'd found a good spot to rob, as they were in nice neighborhoods lined with expensive homes, but then he got to looking and realized that those nice places had security systems and Neighborhood Watch and talkative kids on bicycles who might notice something.

So when he finally found the ideal spot—a piece-of-crap house on the edge of the Everglades—and an ideal pair of marks—two stupid longhairs with modified motorcycles that roared like injured lions, which made them about as inconspicuous as Siegfried and Roy used to be, and who just let people walk in all day and buy drugs—he went to work. If he'd been younger, that would have meant getting city plans of the house, taking pictures of all the angles, maybe even enlisting a getaway car, but at sixty-five, and with these morons, it seemed easier to wait for them to leave for the night, break in through the ceiling—his go-to route, since these guys weren't gonna call the cops anyway, and because there's less absorbent surface to leave fingerprints and such—and rob the place.

Which is exactly what he did.

Two in the morning on a Saturday—your basic come-down time—both morons hopped on their bikes and headed out, messenger bags over their shoulders to make their drops in Miami, and Bruce headed in. Popped through roof tiles into the attic, out through the attic door with a rope ladder and into a bedroom closet, which was good because it was right where he needed to be. File cabinets of paperwork, boxes, bags—actual bags!—of cash. And drugs. Ziplocs filled with crystal meth, crack, pills. It was pitch-dark in the closet and the door was locked from the outside and, smartly, made of steel. On that measure, these boys were wise. Everything else, not so much.

Bruce took all the money, of course. Filled his car

up. And then thought, you know, what drug dealer keeps paperwork? And so he broke back in and took the files, too, thinking he'd have a few more arrows in his quiver. Maybe some car information, house deed . . . who knew? He didn't try to read anything in the dark, just took everything he could and got the hell out, thinking that if his mom got really sick, whatever he found would be worth something to someone. Plus, he really couldn't lose another finger.

"How much money?" Fiona asked.

He hated to tell her, since he had the sense that maybe she'd robbed a few places in the past, too. "Three hundred," he said.

"All of that for three hundred dollars?"

"Thousand," he said. "Three hundred thousand."

"Oh, my," she said. Weird. Maybe she liked him, since her voice took on a much huskier tone. "And when did you find out it was a Ghouls' house?"

"That night when I started going through the paperwork. I didn't even think twice about it then, though," Bruce said, though actually he'd been quite happy. "But then word got back to me that they were looking to find out who would be stupid enough to do the crime, lots of money being thrown around to find out, which meant that soon enough they'd find me. That's why I just want to give what I have back, before they put it all together."

Fiona reached into her bag and pulled out her cell phone. "Anything else you care to add?" she asked.

"Are you single?" he asked. Worth a try.

"I'm free any night for the right price," she said, smiling, "and my price right now includes men with all of their fingers, so you just missed out."

She dialed a number on her phone, still smiling, still giving off one vibe, but clearly not meaning it. She must have robbed banks, Bruce thought.

"Michael," Fiona said, "he's an idiot and he's in trouble, but he's not a liar."

5

Every successful organization, pedestrian or criminal, has a hierarchy. The United States, apart from the occasional hijacked election, is the perfect example of this. Every four years, without violent civil unrest, leadership is allowed to change and, with it, ideology. Countries with dictators also have a hierarchy and within it change also frequently occurs. That change might not include the murderous head of state, but on a local level ministers and department heads move around, different mullahs are favored more than others, and the occasional bureaucrat makes a leap because of a well-timed snitch operation. But belief systems rarely change in dictatorships because no one wants to die for beliefs anymore. Well, unless there's a coup, and then those beliefs are probably the ones people like me have, at some point, put into motion.

Even then there are rules. Break them and people will die, or at least lose their job, or die and lose their job, depending upon just how serious the violation.

You'd think the Ghouls Motorcycle Club wouldn't

have an extensive operating constitution; its members would understand that their jobs were to sell drugs, commit crimes and terrorize people on Honda motorcycles.

You'd be wrong.

Spread across a lovely wicker coffee table that hadn't been dusted since Clinton was in office, there were pages and pages of the Ghouls' rules and regulations, a manual as thick and thorough as the actual constitution. Sam and I sat in the living room of Grossman's house going through the papers, each one stolen in the dark of night from the stash house, while Fiona sat outside with Zadie, apparently having a long conversation concerning *US Magazine*. From my view in the living room, it looked like they were getting along like sisters. That was Fiona's unique ability: She could scare you or charm you, all within a few moments.

"So, just so we're clear," Sam said to Bruce, "you don't want to move to Canada, right?"

I'd called Sam after Fiona told me about Bruce's plight, and now the two of us were trying to figure out how best to keep Bruce alive. Sam's ideas heretofore had also included face-transplant surgery and literally moving underground, like in an old bomb shelter, because trying to elude the grasp of the Ghouls was like trying to catch water in a strainer.

"I can't," he said. "They don't allow ex-felons there."

"I've got a buddy who could get you a very nice passport," Sam said.

Bruce seemed to consider this.

"Says here the Ghouls have an organization in Canada, too," I said. That the official records of the organization were kept in a stash house in the Everglades felt like perpetual stupidity, but then I thought that if I had to look for this information, the last place I'd look would be there, too. And that made sense. Stupid sense, but sense. "In fact, according to this, they have 'colors in all the corners of the world,' which means you better start looking at space travel. You know anyone at NASA, Sam?"

"I could make a call," Sam said.

Bruce exhaled hard from his mouth. Apparently, he didn't care for our line of conversation. "Look," he said, "I can't just disappear. I robbed that place for my mother. If I leave now, who takes care of her? And I'm fifty-five years old."

I looked at him. He sat in a recliner that was probably first purchased so Zadie would have a comfortable seat for the moon landing. But then, the entire house had a dull, antiquated cast to it from all the cigarettes over the years. Lick the sofa and you could probably get a nice nicotine hit.

"Do you want Fiona to come in and talk to you?" I said.

A dash of wonder and pain shot through Grossman's eyes. He did and he didn't. "Okay, fine, sixty-five," he said. "But my point is that I can't start running now. I've never run in my entire life."

"I understand," I said. "But you've put yourself in a position."

"I thought Barry said you knew how to help me, that you were a spy or something," Bruce said.

"That's right," I said. "That doesn't mean I have invisibility potions. If these guys want to find you, Bruce, they will find you."

"Why can't I just mail this stuff back to them? I used to do that all the time."

"So that was you?" I said.

Bruce looked outside toward his mother and Fi but didn't say anything for a minute. "Listen," he said, "my mom? She doesn't know about all that. She thinks I was an architect. And just to be clear, I was never tried for anything but that last job, so I'm not guilty of anything apart from that."

"Which is why the FBI wanted to hire you as a consultant?" I said. "Because you're a failed bank robber?"

"How do you know that?" Bruce asked.

Sam started to say something, but I put a hand up to let him know I still needed to show that I was the alpha in this organizational hierarchy, not that Sam had any idea that was what I was doing. He probably just thought I didn't want to be interrupted. "Let's just say I know things," I said.

"Be that as it may," Bruce said, like he was putting on a show for someone. There was a quality to him that reminded you of a magician, as if every moment might contain a bit of sleight of hand. "I have to stay here. My mother has friends, this is where her doctors are and if this is her last hurrah, I want her to be comfortable. You can understand that, can't you?"

I could and I told him so. "How much money have you spent?" I asked.

"About twenty thousand," he said. "Paid some bills, paid for a nurse for a couple days, bought my mom an air purifier. Probably too late on that one. I haven't opened the mail today, so who knows how much the next bill will be."

"How much does your mom have left? From the finger incident?"

"Not much," he said. "That was twelve years ago. And she's been sick off and on for ten years. Maybe five grand."

"What all did you drop off at the FBI offices?"

Again, a look of shock crossed Bruce's face, but he tried to play it off, or maybe he just realized I really did know things. "A couple role sheets," he said. "Thought if the FBI arrested the crew, they'd be off of me."

"Good idea," Sam said, "but you can't just arrest someone for being an asshole anymore. You actually need to catch them breaking the law. Or breaking their leg while breaking the law. That counts, too."

Bruce shrugged, like: What can you do? You can't do nothing.

"What makes you think they're on to you?" I asked.

"These people have connections everywhere," Bruce said. "They might even have guys in the FBI for all I know."

I was about to say I found that unlikely, but then I thought better of it. If anything is true, it's that every organization has retention and, conversely, leak problems. One person says one thing to the wrong person, and in some cases, an entire spy operation in Moscow could be wiped out. Or a thief in Miami living with his mother could be fingered for a job.

Better to deal with known possibility than wishful thinking.

"Have you told anyone about the job?"

"Just Barry," he said. "He's the one told me they were making inquiries, which got me thinking, you know, don't be a schmuck, get rid of whatever you can and ask for help. Was that wrong?"

"Barry you can trust," I said, already feeling relieved. If he'd told only Barry, we could close the circle, solve the problem, get everyone back to living in peace and harmony and . . .

"And I might have mentioned it to Nick Balsalmo."

He said the name like it should mean something. It didn't. At least not to me. I looked at Sam, whose expression was likewise blank. We all stared at each other for a while, until it became clear none of us was going to offer more information, so Sam finally said, "Of the Miami Balsalmos?"

"We know each other from Glades," Bruce said care-

fully, as if he already knew that it was the wrong thing
to say.

"You *might* have told someone you did time with
that you robbed the Ghouls?" I said. There is no *might*
in these situations, just like I told Barry the previous
day. People either do or don't do things. I had a feeling
I knew the answer.

"Technically," Bruce said, "I didn't know it was the
Ghouls when I told him."

"Well, that's a relief," Sam said. "Or else you *might*
have told him the total truth."

Bruce took off his watch and started rubbing at his
wrist. You spend enough time around people used to
being in handcuffs and you'll begin to notice a similar
compunction when they realize they've put themselves
in a position to be back in cuffs . . . and soon. "I owed
him a favor and knew he could get rid of the drugs I
grabbed," he said. "Just having them in my mother's
home was a *shanda*. Nick is trustworthy. He always
had my back."

If you're sent to prison, it's important to understand
that the people you're doing time with are not, by definition, trustworthy. One of the first rules of incarcera-
tion is simple: Don't owe anybody anything. As soon
as someone has you, they have you forever. This means
inside and outside. You might not know it when it's
happening, but eventually the scales will tip.

"Was Nick Balsalmo part of a prison ministry program?" I asked.

"Uh, no," he said.

"Does Nick Balsalmo work for the police department?" I asked.

"Uh, no," he said again. He was beginning to get the path of this line of questioning.

"Does he work in hazardous waste disposal?"

"No."

"No," I said. "No, I'm going to guess Nick Balsalmo is a drug dealer. Would that be an accurate description?"

"More like a courier. He doesn't sell on the streets. I couldn't trust a guy who sold drugs to kids or something."

"Of course not," I said. "Who could?"

The sarcasm was lost on Bruce.

"Right, right, my feeling exactly. But he works with bigger businesses, I guess you could say."

"A middleman," Sam offered.

"Exactly, exactly," Bruce said. "A middleman."

"So it might stand to reason that Mr. Balsalmo would be in the business of selling your stolen drugs to people who suddenly found themselves, say, low on product? Would that sound plausible?" I said.

"Uh, yes," Bruce said. And there it was. Dawning.

"When did you speak with him last?"

"Three, four days ago. He called to thank me. Said he was having good luck moving the stuff, wanted to know if I wanted, you know, a cut. I said no, of course."

"Of course," Sam said.

"Of course," I said. I gave him a big smile and then

said, "You might want to give him a call. See if he's still alive."

The color left Bruce's face then. He'd known this was serious before, certainly, but for some reason he hadn't seen all of the consequences of his actions. I tossed him my cell phone and he dialed Nick's number on speaker. After a few rings, an automated voice announced that the voice mail was full.

"What kind of drug dealer doesn't check his messages?" I said.

"Maybe he's out of town?" Bruce said.

"That's why people have voice mail, Bruce, so they can get their calls anywhere. Especially drug dealers. Do you know where he lives?"

"He lives with a Cuban girl out in Little Havana. I went over there for dinner once. Nice place." There was a matter-of-factness to Bruce that sometimes felt very odd: He was essentially a very simple guy. For a person who did twelve years, he didn't seem to be all that jaded, or damaged, which meant that for some reason he hadn't had a terrible experience in jail. Or not as terrible as others.

"What did you owe Nick for, exactly?"

Bruce got a pensive look on his face and started rubbing at his wrist again. When he finally spoke, it was just above a whisper. "He did my finger."

"Could you speak up, Bruce?" Sam said. "I can't quite hear you. Ten percent hearing loss in my right ear from the Falklands."

Bruce didn't know quite what to make of Sam, so for a moment he glared at him in a rather benign way, as if to say, You could say please. It didn't last. "He did my finger, okay? Spent two months in the hole for it. When he got out, there was this *meshugass* with my mother's illness, and so I couldn't pay him what I owed him initially, but he was cool, really. The dinner and all that. Ever had Cuban pork chops? Authentic Cuban pork chops?"

"Once," I said.

"Where?"

"In Santiago de Cuba," I said.

"But I thought that . . ." He stopped for a minute, thought about where he was going, opted to change lanes. "Anyway, he was perfectly sweet about everything, but it was clear he wanted what was his."

"Let me get this right," Sam said. "Guy takes off *your* finger and *you* have to pay *him*? That's inflation for you. Mikey, you hear that?"

"I hear that," I said.

"It doesn't make sense on the outside, I know," Bruce said. "But it's a different set of rules in prison."

"How much did you owe him?" I asked.

"Fifty grand," he said.

"How much do you think he could get for the drugs you gave him?"

"Enough that he felt comfortable offering me a cut," Bruce said.

"Real gentleman," Sam said.

The problem here was that even if Bruce wanted to give the Ghouls back their drugs—presuming Nick hadn't already tried to sell them their own stuff—a good sum of it was already gone. And I didn't feel comfortable giving anyone back a bunch of drugs—there's no way into that situation that is safe and I didn't particularly want to kill anyone that week. Or be killed, for that matter.

"Nick, he's a good guy," Bruce said. "He just has a bad job. But who doesn't?"

Bruce made a convincing argument, but it might just have been his delivery. Having a sixty-five-year-old man give you a slice of prison wisdom does have a certain charm. He wanted to explain more, but before he could, Fiona came to the sliding glass window and cracked it open.

"Zadie would like something to eat," she said to Bruce, who jumped from his seat like he'd been shocked and went directly into caregiver mode, rushing off to the other side of the great room and into the kitchen to fix his mother a sandwich.

Sam and I both watched him for a bit, how meticulous he was in putting together a plate for her, how he put the sandwich in one corner, a bit of Jell-O in another, how he washed by hand a few leaves of lettuce and then shook pepper onto them, followed by a dash of oil and vinegar. He then poured his mother an entire glass of ginger ale, no ice.

"We have to help him," I said quietly.

Sam nodded once.

Bruce walked past us to the patio without saying a word.

"A complication," Sam said, still watching Bruce. "Before I got here I ran the information on the house he hit. It was burned down last night."

"Not a surprise," I said.

"With the occupants inside of it," Sam said.

"How many?"

"Two. But I wouldn't be surprised if they found this Balsalmo in a ditch in the back if he's as savvy as our friend Bruce is."

Page ten of the Ghouls' constitution said, "You dishonor the Ghouls. The price is determined by your dishonor."

I guess they meant it.

Trying to figure out how to return stolen property is like trying to un-swallow: There's no actual opposite action that will return the property (or the food you've eaten) in its original form. There will always be an elemental difference. Steal from someone and even if they get their stuff back in whole cloth, they're still going to feel that sense of violation. Steal from a criminal organization and whether or not they feel violated, they're going to want revenge.

In Bruce Grossman's case, he didn't actually want to return everything he'd stolen. He wanted to keep the money and give back the drugs and the paperwork and the box of patches that he'd also lifted and just call it even, which wasn't going to work. There's no even when three hundred thousand bucks is left out of the equation. And stealing a gang's patches is maybe worst of all. It's silly, but these grown men live and die for a stitch of cloth.

"Here's what I don't get," Sam said. We were back at my loft. I was eating blueberry yogurt. Fiona was doing this thing where she sits quietly flipping through a fashion magazine but is really listening to everything and waiting to make proclamations that will solve all the problems we've encountered. Sam was doing what Sam does: drinking my beer and asking questions. "If you're a criminal mastermind, like Bruce thinks he is, why would you be so stupid?"

"He's not a criminal mastermind," I said, "so that solves that."

"He's closer to a criminal mastermind than either of you are," Fiona said. She didn't even bother to look up from her magazine.

"Because we're not criminals," I said.

"Have you ever tried to break into a safe-deposit box?" she asked.

Sam and I looked at each other. She had a point. Kind of.

"I've cracked into a few secure locations," Sam said. "And Mikey here could have Fort Knox renamed Fort Westen in no time. Right, Mikey?"

"Uh, right," I said.

Fiona was heading somewhere. This was just the opening salvo. She raised her eyebrows, but kept her eyes on the magazine, turning pages casually. "I should have been a model," she said to no one in particular. "Seems like I'd get to sit around on bearskin rugs in Uggs and a bikini, not a care in the world."

"Is there something you want to tell me?" I said.

"Is there something you want to tell me?" Fiona said.

"I think it's cute when you guys repeat each other's sentences," Sam said.

"Do you know who Bruce Grossman is, Michael?" Fiona said. "I mean, do you really know?"

"I know he's a person with a problem," I said. "I know he's a friend of Barry's. I know he's been a fool since he got out of prison. I know his mother is going to die soon. Isn't that enough?"

Fiona shook her head slowly, like she couldn't believe how utterly daft I was. "Right, right," she said. She still hadn't bothered to put down the magazine or look at either me or Sam. "What I'm saying is that the man is near a legend, Michael. I heard of what he was doing in Ireland. He broke into every bank imaginable. And so smart about it, too. Safe-deposit boxes are bank robber nirvana, Michael."

"And?"

"And maybe he'd be good to keep around," Fiona said. She looked up finally, smiling, flirting, batting eyelashes, doing that thing she does with the tip of her tongue along the inside of her bottom lip.

"No," I said.

"No, what?"

I could see the wheels turning in her mind.

"No, he will not rob banks with you. No, you will not sell his services to other people who rob banks. No, you will not put him in a box and ship him to a small town in Iceland where there are very old banks. No, no and no."

There's not much about Fiona that remains a mystery to me, apart from her total nihilism. But it's unusually cute, so there's that.

"I'm just saying that in the position you're in," she said, "where revenue streams seem inconsistent, it might be wise to look at all avenues, Michael. It's not every day someone from history shows up."

"Duly noted," I said, "and still, no."

I went back to eating my yogurt and thinking about how to un-swallow Bruce's problems. Fiona went back to reading her magazine, presumably thinking about the fashion shoots she'd missed in Bora Bora all these years. But Sam wasn't doing anything. That was troubling, particularly since he'd finished his beer and hadn't gone foraging in my fridge for another.

"Is he really from history?" Sam asked.

"The Safe-Deposit Bandit," Fiona said. "There are probably textbooks about him."

"As a kid, I always thought it was 'safety' deposit box," Sam said.

"That's because your American education never put

the proper emphasis on enunciation. Both of you sound like you learned to speak with dirt in your mouth."

Sam gave me a look that said, basically, What the hell?

"Something else troubling you, Fiona?"

"If you must know," she said, "I'd like it if you found a way to describe me that didn't make me sound like the help."

"That's my cue," Sam said and headed for the door.

"Wait," I said. "We haven't figured out what we're going to do with Bruce."

"I can't stand to hear you two fight," Sam said, already halfway out the door of my loft. "It just breaks my heart."

"Sam," I said.

All that was left was his waving arm. "Call me later," he shouted. "We'll do some covert stuff together and it will be a great time."

And then he was gone completely, leaving me alone with Fiona, who, in the last year or so, had become an inconsistent emotional concern. One minute she loved me, the next minute she hated me, a minute after that she was kissing me, two minutes later she was punching me in the head, five minutes later we were in bed . . . and always, always, there was some guilt on both ends.

And now this.

"If we're going to talk about this," I said, "you're going to need to put that magazine down."

"If I do that," she said, perfectly calm, "I might be inclined to use it as a weapon."

"Fine," I said. I sat down on my bed, across from the chair she was sitting in. "Let's hear it."

"Well," she said, "do you consider me your friend or your associate?"

"Yes, technically, I believe both are accurate descriptions."

Fiona hurled the magazine at me, but fortunately she hadn't slipped a sharp piece of broken glass into the pages beforehand, which is a nice trick if you want to really hurt someone. So the magazine just fluttered to the ground.

"Wrong answer," she said.

"Fi, look, I'm not comfortable categorizing who we are to complete strangers, particularly not people like Bruce Grossman. He's not exactly a confidential source."

"I'm not speaking of him solely," she said. "It would just be nice if, every now and then, I knew where I stood before I was offended by your boorish behavior."

"Okay," I said, thinking, I have no idea where we stand, moment to moment. "How would you like me to describe you?"

Fiona stood up then, went into my kitchen, poured water into a teapot and began preparing a cup of tea. It was as if I wasn't even in the room. I watched her for a few moments, the simple, fluid motions of her actions, the lack of wasted space she conveyed. After about five minutes, the water came to a boil and she fixed her tea. She sat back down in her chair and played absently with the steeping teabag. "Any ideas come to you yet, Michael?" she asked.

"A few," I said.

"Good," she said. "Remember them when next the moment arises."

I nodded. "In the meantime"—I paused—"most elegant Fiona"—I paused again, to see how that went over; well, it turns out—"we need to figure out what to do with Bruce Grossman."

"How much time do you presume he has left until the Ghouls figure out who did the job?" she asked. "Assuming Balsalmo didn't tell them?"

"How many people living in Miami that they don't already know *could* do the job?" I said. "Someone in Miami, other than Barry, other than Balsalmo, likely knows who Bruce Grossman is, especially if you did and you're not even from these here parts."

"Then maybe you should just go tell them before they find out."

"You *are* elegant," I said.

"I know," Fi said. She got up from her seat again and poured her tea down the drain.

"You just made that," I said.

"Merely as an instructional tool," she said. She looked at her watch. "Have you called your mother lately?"

"No."

"You should," she said, "seeing as I am the only person who has the kindness to actually return her calls."

"What does she have you doing?"

"I've agreed to take her shopping for lamps this afternoon."

"You have fun with that," I said.

She walked over and kissed me once on the cheek. "Thank you," she said.

"For what?"

"For watching," she said, "and for wanting to watch."

Sometimes, just like a real person, all Fiona wants is to be appreciated.

After Fiona left, I called Sam. "That was fast," he said.

"You just have to know the right words," I said.

"I'm not even at the Carlito yet. Right words or not, I figured this for a good day-or-two-long fight. Maybe with injuries. You have all of your limbs?"

"Present and accounted for."

"She even hit you?"

"Not this time," I said.

"She's full of surprises," Sam said. "When she does hit you, though, that actually hurts, right?"

"It never feels good to get punched, Sam." Sam started to respond, but I stopped him before he could begin exalting again the pleasures of the Flying Lotus, and instead I asked, "How long would it take for you to get your hands on a few bikes?"

"I got a guy I could talk to," he said.

"Talk to him," I said.

"How many?"

"Two," I said.

"Sidecars?"

"This isn't World War Two, Sam."

"If we're planning a full frontal assault here, Mikey, we might want to plan for every contingency."

"I don't see us needing sidecars," I said. "No matter the contingency."

"I'll look into it. They had them at the last inauguration. Looked pretty sharp, Mikey, can't deny that."

"Not really the look I'm aiming for."

"What's the plan here? Shock and awe or more spit and shine?"

I told him Fiona's idea—delivering Grossman, or at least delivering his identity, and maybe some of his stolen goods—to the Ghouls, and then that way we could control the situation. What that situation happened to be depended upon how much they already knew.

"First thing, though," I said, "I need to look into the mortality of Nick Balsalmo. If he's alive, we need to make sure he stays that way and stays quiet."

"Gotcha," he said. "I suppose just UPSing the Ghouls their stuff is out of the question."

"Not going to work," I said. "That's why we need the bikes."

"We're talking choppers only here? That the look you want?"

"Right," I said.

"Chuck Finley rides again," Sam said and hung up.

When you're dealing with motorcycle gangs, you have to understand that they aren't like normal criminals. It's an entire culture—a culture that demands loyalty above all else; and if that means someone has to die for merely being negligent, that's not a problem. It also means if you disrespect them, it's like disrespecting Hezbollah: They will fight you forever, wherever.

In order to help Bruce out, it wouldn't be as simple as giving the Ghouls back what was taken. We'd have to direct them to something larger than Bruce. Another gang. A snitch within their ranks. Someone directing Bruce's actions for something bigger, more destructive. Get them thinking Bruce was just an instrument and they'd focus their attention on fighting that war. I'd need to get close to them to figure out just what that trigger might be.

In the meantime, we just had to keep Bruce and his mother safe. And that I had a plan for.

I looked at my watch. Not enough time had elapsed, so I did some push-ups, a few sit-ups, a hundred crunches and some light tae kwon do in the mirror. When it seemed like Fi would have had enough time to cross the city, pick up my mom and then head off to Lamps Are Us, I called my mother's house.

"Ma," I said into her answering machine (a Record-A-Call from 1979, to be precise), "I have some friends I'd like you to meet. I'll bring them by around dinnertime. You're just going to love them both."

6

Urban warfare isn't any fun. Ask any soldier what they'd prefer and they'll tell you that a clear, fixed target on a battlefield with a linear objective, replete with a front and a rear, is much easier to control than going door-to-door in a burned-out city. Gettysburg or Fallujah, basically, and if you're a betting man and you're betting on your life, you'll take Gettysburg every time.

Problem is, no one fights conventionally anymore. They've all seen *Black Hawk Down* and *Full Metal Jacket*, they've all watched CNN and Al Jazeera and they all play first-person shooter video games. Thus they all know that fighting inside buildings and alleys is the great equalizer to light manpower.

So when you're in a densely packed urban environment and looking for possibly hostile targets, it's wise to look as nonthreatening as possible. Most spies spend their whole lives in slacks and a button-down shirt. It doesn't matter if they are working in the Pentagon or Darfur: Slacks and a button-down shirt are almost always plain enough to be completely unnoticeable, because when you're a spy it's important never to dress to bring attention. You want to blend in.

On the rare occasion you need a disguise, it's imperative to remember that it's easier to look older than younger, poorer than richer and that if you want people to think you have a limp, put a rock in your shoe. That way, you'll actually limp.

So when I went to the apartment of Nick Balsalmo's girlfriend in Little Havana, I tried to look as innocuous as possible, since I wasn't sure if I was going to stumble onto a dead body, or a booby trap or a bunch of bikers waiting to kill whoever showed up at his house. I opted for jeans, a T-shirt, a straw hat and ugly shoes with no socks. Looking obviously lost is a good way to avoid trouble, even in a war zone.

I also had two guns on me, because there's never been a single person who thought being overly armed was a bad thing. When you're not sure how many bullets you might need, bring as many as you can hold.

Little Havana is just that: little. Densely packed with businesses, shops, bars, the streets of Little Havana feel like they've been cut and pasted into Miami from any of a dozen towns in Cuba. Salsa and merengue bleat through cars and the open windows of small apartments above storefronts and there seems to be an open-air restaurant on every corner.

For the most part, Little Havana is safe. There are plenty of families, which means people tend to look out for their own, but then there's also plenty of Families, too, so the crime in Little Havana can be organized and brutal. That Nick Balsalmo, who wasn't Cuban, was living in Little Havana with his girlfriend didn't necessarily mean that he was being protected, but a guy like him living in the same neighborhood as Cuban crime families meant something.

The address Bruce gave me was a three-story stucco apartment building not far from the domino park off of Calle Ocho where, even though it was getting late in the afternoon, old-timers in guayaberas were still throwing bones and whooping at one another. On one side of the building was a liquor store and on the other was a cigar shop and then two doors down there was a McDonald's and a Domino's. That was the weird thing about Little Havana—it looked like Cuba apart from how much it looked like any neighborhood in Anytown, U.S.A.

Nick and his girlfriend—whom Bruce only knew as Maria—lived on the second floor of the building. The front door of the building was locked and required the person living in the apartment to buzz you up, so I found Maria's name and hit the button. The system rang their number and a mechanical voice announced that their voice mail was full.

Not a good sign.

The door had an electric strike lock activated by discontinuing the electrical circuit by hitting a number (or a series of numbers) on the phone's keypad. These locks usually confound people intent on breaking in because they don't understand how easy they are to break. Most electric strike locks in older buildings are fail-safe, which means they need electricity to stay locked, which gives you two easy options:

Find the electrical path to the door in the wall and yank out the cords.

Go to the side of the building, find the power box, and turn off the power. You might need to pick the padlock on the box, but as long as you have two paper clips, this should take only about five seconds.

Or you can do what I did: Wait three minutes for a young woman to walk out the door, smile at her, say "thanks" and she will hold the door open for you while you gather your materials and walk inside. The nice thing about people is that they are usually very polite and helpful, even when letting perfect strangers into their home.

I climbed a flight of stairs to the second-floor landing and made my way down the hall. There were six apartments on the floor and all of them, except for the one at the end of the hall, had their front doors wide open. As I passed each one, I could hear the drone of televisions, the cacophony of too many people in a small space having arguments and the wail of more than one child. I peered into each apartment and was struck by how similar they looked—a galley kitchen opening into a large living room, which opened onto an outdoor balcony. I could smell cooking meat and deep-fried vegetables, human sweat and something that smelled vaguely like vinegar, but more pungent.

The closer I got to the last apartment, however, the more I began to notice a different smell.

A smell that reminded me of Kosovo. Of Iraq. Of Afghanistan.

You never get used to the smell of decomposing people. Smell it once and no amount of deodorizer or lye or bleach will hide the smell from your nose for too long. Dead bodies smell like rotten lamb, and fecal matter, and rotten fruit, and spoiled milk, wrapped in burning garbage, but worse. Dead people smell like no other dead animal for simple evolutionary purposes. It gets the living moving . . . and fast.

In this case, however, someone had gone a long way to hide the smell, because as I stood outside the door, I could decipher it only as an undertone. My guess was that whoever was dead inside the apartment—and my guess was that it was probably both Nick and Maria, because biker gangs aren't known for leaving witnesses—was being absorbed by an acid, probably in the bathtub.

"You know the guy who lives there?"

I turned and saw a balding man of about fifty. He had about fifty keys on a belt chain and wore a short-sleeved work shirt that was pocked with sweat across the chest. It said RAY in cursive over the breast pocket. I had the sense that he wore this shirt every day but didn't bother to wash it.

"Know him? No," I said. "Just know that he owes me money."

Ray nodded but didn't say anything. He looked me up and down once but didn't convey any emotion.

"Have you seen him?" I asked.

"I'm not sure," he said. "I don't normally answer questions from people dressed like you carrying two guns but who have to sneak into my building."

Interesting.

"Jackie Roach," I said, extending my hand. The man shook it but didn't put much effort behind it. He wanted to hear my story. I had one. I always have one. "I work for the banks, tracking down people who've skipped on their foreclosures. Mr. Balsalmo, he owes Seminole Savings and Loan a considerable amount of money." I pulled up my shirt and showed him the locations of my two guns, which he really shouldn't have been able to see, but I had the sense that this guy had been around a gun or two in his time. "You gotta protect yourself when you have my job. You understand?"

"I understand," he said, and lifted up his left pant leg, revealing a Saturday night special in an ankle holster. "You do property management for long? Packing is just like brushing your teeth in the morning."

"Been there, done that, bought the bootleg off eBay!" I said and gave the man a full belly laugh. "One thing Jackie Roach knows is property management. Doing God's work, buddy, God's work."

Ray still wasn't smiling, still wasn't exactly happy to

see me and still didn't know quite what to make of me. Being a property manager is a lot like being a prison guard: You see all kinds of miscreants on a day-to-day basis and everyone lies to you.

"You got a letter or something you want to leave?"

"Letters don't work anymore," I said. "You know that. It's all about face-to-face with these people. That personal connection. Gotta be close enough to strangle someone to get your point across, right?"

Still nothing from Ray. He was listening to me, but it was as if he was trying to hear another conversation at the same time. Like he was looking for the subtext.

"Unless you got something," he said eventually, "maybe you should just head on out. People in this building work for a living, someone like you in the building scares them, you understand? People got kids in here. We don't need any more drama. Get it?"

I did. And "it" was not good. And accounted for the smell, too, I'd guess. I took a step toward Ray and leaned in a bit. "Look, this Balsalmo guy was bad news, right? Did a little time. Dealt some crank. I understand. I saw his record. I get that. I got kids, too, right? But, Machito, I'm just doing my job. Maybe you open the door and just see if he's hiding in there? If he is, I have a conversation with him and then I go."

Ray shifted his weight from foot to foot, as if he were literally weighing his options, but didn't say anything. Having a conversation with Ray required one to fill in a lot of blanks.

"His girl been around at all? Maria? Because maybe I could talk to her. She was always the reasonable one."

The mention of Maria's name got Ray animated. "She moved out last week. Let him keep the place. Put him on the lease and everything. Stupid, eh? Italian guy living in Little Havana. You knew he didn't have a clue."

A little boy came running down the hall, screaming at full throat. Not like he was hurt. Like he was a little boy. But when he saw Ray, he came to a full and silent stop.

"Sorry, Mr. Ray," the boy said, before hustling inside one of the open doors.

Ray started walking toward the door and shuffling keys. "Nick, he's a nice guy. Respectful to me. 'Sir' this and 'sir' that, but he's not the kind of element I want in my building. So maybe we just have a talk with him together. You up for that?"

"Ray, I'm one hundred percent up for that," I said. "Nice people got bad debts and got bad jobs. But I got kids, like I said, so I know what you're saying."

Ray put his key in the door and started knocking at the same time, saying, "It's Ray," as loud as he could. "It's Ray. I got Jackie Roach with me. It's Ray," he said one more time and then opened the door. He turned to me before he stepped in. "You smell that?"

"Maybe a dead rat?" I said, which was probably true, just not in the same context.

"That ain't a rat," he said.

Nick Balsalmo's apartment looked like a Jackson Pollock painting. Spatter patterns on the ceiling, the walls, the floor. Pools of blood in the living room. From the angles and velocity, it appeared he'd been bludgeoned as the final coda, but the pools indicated he'd also just bled a lot, like, say, if his fingers had been cut off. Ray walked through the apartment briskly, opening doors while I stood in the entry hall surveying the scene. I hadn't touched anything yet and wasn't about to. I just needed to hear Ray say what I already knew: Somewhere, Nick Balsalmo's body was rotting away under some chemical.

"Oh, Jesus," Ray shrieked. "Oh, Jesus," he said again. "He's in here!" It sounded like Ray was in the bathroom, though it was hard to tell as I was already back down the hall and heading for the exit. Nick Balsalmo was dead. What I didn't need was to be standing there when the police came, trying to explain who I was.

After I got to my car and zipped back into late-afternoon Miami gridlock, I called Barry. I had to try five different numbers, but I finally found him.

"Where are you?" I said when he answered.

"In a comfortable spiritual place," he said, his voice just above a whisper.

"Listen to me," I said. "You're in danger. Tell me where you are and I'll pick you up."

"I'm in a church, Mike," he said.

"What are you doing in a church?"

"I'm meeting a business associate."

"In a church?"

"Do you know how hard it is to get a legal bug into a church? It's sanctuary space. Plus, my business associate works here."

"You're washing money for a church?"

"Tough times, Mike. Even the Lord has to eat."

Negotiating cramped Miami traffic and the cramped logic of Barry at the same time wasn't something I was prepared for. "Do you know Nick Balsalmo?"

"I know his work."

"He's dead," I said.

"He's in a better place, then," Barry said. "Praise the Lord."

"Your friend Bruce gave him the drugs he got from the Ghouls' stash house."

"Why would he do that?"

"He had to pay him off for a prison favor and the Ghouls' drugs worked out well for that," I said. "I have a feeling the Ghouls found that upsetting."

"There were plenty of people who'd like to kill Nick Balsalmo. He sold drugs for a living. It's a very unstable work environment. Praise the Lord."

"Barry," I said, "there was more of him on the outside than on the inside. I'm going to guess that whatever someone wanted to get from Nick, they got. Maybe that included your name, maybe it didn't, but I'm going to guess known associates of Bruce Grossman might be wise to keep a low profile."

"Praise the Lord."

"Really?"

"I'm just trying to fit in over here," Barry said, his voice low again. "I sit in a pew talking on a cell phone in here, people might find that disrespectful."

"But laundering their money is right with God?"

"No sin in getting ahead."

I thought that was actually wrong, canonically, but opted not to press Barry on the issue. "I'm picking Bruce and his mom up and taking them somewhere safe. I'm happy to extend you the same courtesy. Consider it a returned favor for this great job you found for me."

"Fortress inside of a moon crater?"

"My mother's house," I said.

"That's sweet," Barry said, "but I've got a safe house. It's called a boat. On the Atlantic. Do you know how hard it is to drive a motorcycle over water?"

"What's also nice is that no one can hear you screaming on the Atlantic, either."

Barry didn't respond for a while, so I just sat there and listened to him breathe. It was sounding a bit more labored than usual. He's not a skinny guy, but he's also not one of those wheezing fat guys, either. I definitely noticed a quickening of his intake, however.

"I've got a sick friend in Montana I could visit," he said.

"Try one of the Dakotas," I said.

"I hear South Dakota is nice this time of year."

"Don't limit yourself," I said. "Try them both."

"Mike, you're scaring me here."

"Praise the Lord," I said. "That's what I'm trying to do."

Barry was silent again. In the background I could hear an organ being played. Maybe he was already in heaven.

"When you say there was more of Balsalmo on the outside than the inside," Barry said, "you meant that literally, right?"

"Yes."

Silence.

More organ music.

"I don't vacation enough," Barry said.

"No time like the present."

"You'll call me if, you know, there's something I need to know?"

"I will."

"And maybe now would be a good time to use an alias?"

"Now would be that time, yes."

Silence again. I've never thought of Barry as a particularly pensive guy.

"You need money or something?" he asked. He sounded hopeful again. If there's one thing Barry knows, it's money.

"I'm fine, Barry. Down the line, I'm sure we'll tip the scales again."

"I appreciate that, Mike," Barry said.

"Future reference," I said, "I'd like to avoid going to war with a biker gang."

"Praise the Lord," Barry said.

"Praise the Lord," I said and hung up.

7

There is no such thing as a safe house. Any fixed location is, by definition, a waiting target. Hide long enough and no matter how safe you feel, you will eventually begin to create a traceable root system. It doesn't matter if you're in a log cabin in Lincoln, Montana, or a spider hole outside of Tikrit, stay in one place long enough and the people looking for you will find you.

If you really want to ensure that no one can find you, you have to keep moving. Adhere to three simple rules and maybe you'll live long enough to outlast whoever is chasing you:

1. Never spend more than twenty-four hours in the same place.
2. Pay cash for everything.
3. Sleep during the day, travel during the night.

Even still, this plan requires financial resources and unwavering determination. There is nothing more exhausting or emotionally isolating than constantly running for your life. So if you choose to embark on this kind of life, expect that your interpersonal relationships will suffer.

Despite all that, if you have to stay safe for just one or two days and you have ample protection—say, if a burned spy is watching over you—it's important to fortify your position and not merely assume that by being out of sight you are somehow safer than if you were parading down A1-A with a target painted on your chest.

Which is why I was outside my mother's house laying tactical wire across the backyard, Sam was placing protective wire through my mother's rosebushes and Fiona was working on the roof. Inside, my mother had just served Bruce and Zadie her patented "light dinner"—pot roast, garlic mashed potatoes and a pasta salad whose main secondary ingredient was mayonnaise—though she kept coming outside to smoke and complain.

"Michael, you know I don't like meeting strangers," my mother said. She'd just stepped out onto the back porch and was watching me with unique disinterest. Having me fortify her home had become a frequent activity of late.

"They're nice people, Ma," I said.

"Zadie told me confidentially that her son was just in prison, Michael!"

"Everyone lives somewhere," I said.

"He is very cute, though," she said. I decided to try

to unhear that by simply not reacting to it. "And, Michael, not being able to smoke inside my own home is making me very nervous."

"Ma," I said, "Zadie is dying of cancer. You recognize that smoking causes cancer, right?"

"Allegedly," she said.

It was the early evening, which meant the sidewalks around my mother's house had already been rolled up for the night. The only signs of life on the street apart from the three of us fortifying our positions were the odd appearances and sounds of Reagan-era Lincoln Continentals and Chryslers slipping into garages throughout the neighborhood.

Early-bird specials live on in Miami.

I was trying to maintain a level of calm and appreciation for my mother, seeing as she was doing me a tactical favor, and in light of the houseguests, so I opted not to counter the "alleged" claim.

"I'm just feeling very jumpy, Michael. I don't like worrying about the guests and worrying about who might attack the house and, on top of it all, worrying about when I can have another cigarette."

"That's the nice thing about smoking," I said. "Do it long enough and you won't have to worry about it anymore. You'll just be dead."

"Michael, you don't need to give me your speech. I see those public service announcements."

I stepped away from my mother and strung wire about a foot off of the ground from the side of the garage to the bougainvillea climbing up the fence that separated Mom's house from the neighbor's. Technically, the backyard was a friendly zone, meaning that if you happened to be sitting in the kitchen and saw someone trying to climb the back fence and break into the house through the backyard, the advantage was yours. The only actual exit to open safety was through the house or back over the fence. With the wire only twenty feet from the house, anyone coming that close would fall and likely slice themselves up in the process, which would be painful, but only until they were shot by the sniper watching them from inside.

Or my brother, Nate, with a shotgun. He was in town, visiting from Las Vegas for the week, and was coming over that night to help out. All I'd had to tell him was that his job was protecting a bank robber from a vicious biker gang and he signed on immediately.

When I finished stringing the wire, I walked back to where my mother stood. She was already on her second cigarette.

"Have you seen Zadie, Ma? Is that how you want to end up?"

"Michael, I need tar. It's actually very helpful for my fibromyalgia."

"You don't have fibromyalgia," I said.

"How do you know? People don't just hurt. Something must be wrong with me."

"Where do you hurt, Ma?"

She waved her hand over an area roughly the equivalent of her entire torso. "It's worse in the morning," she said.

"Maybe you should buy a new mattress," I said.

"There's nothing wrong with the one I have," she said. "I've slept on it since the week you were born."

Luckily, before I could respond, Sam came through the gate into the yard. He stepped over the wire lines adroitly. If you know what to look for, it's easy not to get tripped up.

"Mikey, you want razors on the wire in the bushes?" Sam said.

I actually heard my mother gasp.

"Yes," I said. It's an instinctual thing. My mother disapproves, I immediately approve.

"Michael, what about the gardeners?" my mother said.

"When do they come?" Sam asked.

"Well, I don't know, Sam," she said.

"Do you *have* gardeners, Ma?"

"There's a neighbor boy," she said. "He reminds me so much of you and Nate when you were his age."

"He's forced labor, too?" I said. My mother stuck her cigarette back into her mouth and fixed her jaw in the way she does when she wants to convey anger, hurt, disappointment and incredulity.

"So that's a yes, Mikey?"

"That's a yes," I said. "Anyone gets close enough to the house that they're in the bushes, they're in the wrong place."

Sam nodded. But then, because he's Sam, and maybe a better person than me as it relates to my mother, he said, "Are you all right with that, Madeline?"

"Whatever James Bond says," she said and then tossed her cigarette down, ground it out with the tip of her shoe and stormed back inside. She slammed the door and everything. I stood there for a moment staring at the door. The sound of it slamming in my face was oddly reminiscent of a period of my life I like to call "childhood."

"Awkward," Sam said.

"You have now seen my entire youth in a split second," I said. "Any news on the bikes?"

Sam checked his watch. "Yeah, I have to meet a guy in about an hour. Did some Donnie Brasco work with the Ghouls back in the nineties, owes me a favor or two, so he's hooking me up with a couple choppers. What's Fiona gonna ride?"

I looked up at the roof. Fiona was busy stretching a wire around all of the vents and across the chimney. I'd need to remind myself of this when Christmas rolled around, lest I chop off a foot putting Santa and Rudolph up.

"Yes," I said. "About that. I spent some time reading their constitution. Women are, technically, property, according to the Ghouls. We bring her with us, I'm going to need to convince her that for this job, she'll need to pretend like I'm her master."

"Sounds difficult," Sam said.

"Yes. But I think I can put a life-or-death spin on it and Fi will react well."

Sam just nodded. And nodded. And nodded some more. "I'd work through that whole scenario in your head a few more times before you bring it up to Fi."

"I will. But, uh, she'll be riding on the back of my bike. No sidecars, right?"

"Mikey, it's a chance of a lifetime we're missing here."

"We roll up on the Ghouls, we have to do it right. Way I've read it, there's only one way of attacking this problem."

"Lots of pyrotechnics?"

"You need to spend less time with Fiona," I said.

"I've warmed up to some of her views on conflict resolution," he said.

"She'd have us burn down the Everglades to root out an alligator."

"That's what we did to Saddam," Sam said.

"And look how that turned out, Sam," I said. "In the meantime, find out from your friend where the Ghouls congregate. Not just their public clubhouse, but maybe where they make their meth, hold their area meetings and design their next Boy Scout badge. If my plan works, we'll need both."

"Got it," Sam said.

The back door opened then and Bruce's mother, Zadie, stepped out before I could continue with the plan. She hadn't said much since I'd picked her up a few hours ago, but then she didn't look like she had the energy to do much complaining about anything. She was completely bald and kept her head covered with a turban. Her skin had a translucent quality to it.

"How are we doing, Zadie?" I said.

"I'm not deaf," she said.

"Of course you aren't," I said.

"Then why are you shouting at me?"

"Am I shouting?" I turned to Sam and then back to her. Both were just staring at me. Apparently I was being loud. "Sorry," I said. "Habit. Tough to get through to my mother, you see."

"Your mother is trying to kill me," she said.

"The smoke?" I said.

"The dinner."

"Just take a jog," Sam said. "Work all those complex fats right out of you."

Zadie was wearing a sweat suit, but didn't look much like the jogging type.

"I came out here to ask you a question," she said to me.

"Ask away."

"Did Bruce do something stupid again?"

"No," I said.

"You know I'm eighty-eight," she said. "I can handle the truth."

I looked at Sam, but he was attempting to appear transfixed by a leaf. "It's a complex issue," I said. "He had good intentions."

"My son, always with the good intentions." She shook her head a few times. "His father, my husband, may he rest in peace, was the same way."

"Your husband robbed banks, too?" I asked. When you're dealing with someone who has been alive for eighty-eight years, it's wise to just come clean. Skirting around the corners of things is for the young and the restless.

"Buses," she said.

"Buses?" Sam said. Now he was engaged.

"Buses?" I said.

"Those muni buses, back before everyone had a pass, carried a lot of cash on them."

"A lot of coins," Sam said.

"Coins are money, too."

"What about you, Zadie?" I said. "Ever turn over a liquor store?"

"My husband and my son," she said, a derisive tone rising in her voice. "No sense between them. Me, I understood a hard day's work." She explained that after her husband died in 1965 from a heart attack, she worked first as a teller at a bank, moved all the way up to assistant manager, but had to quit when her son was accused of walking out with some property.

"Property?" I said. "So that would be money?"

"Someone said he took a roll of quarters," she said. "Never proved. Who's to say he didn't have ten dollars in quarters in his pocket to start with?"

"Who is to say?" Sam agreed. "She's got a point there, Mikey."

Mothers want to think the best of their sons. This isn't spycraft. It's just common sense. No one who's had another human living inside of them for nine months hopes to believe that human is a detestable waste of carbon.

Not Zadie.

Not my mother.

Not Fiona's or Sam's or anyone's.

"Your son did what any good child would do, Mrs. Grossman," I said. "He just tried to take care of his mother. He ran into a little problem in the process of it all, but it's going to work out. In the meantime, you'll stay here for a few days, my mother will order takeout, we'll drive you to your doctor's appointments and everyone will sleep easier when it's over."

"And that's why you're running razor wire around this house?" she said.

"Yes," I said.

She reached up and squeezed my cheek. "You're a smart boychik," she said. And then she squeezed a little harder. "Don't get me killed. I'm already dying, okay?"

"Okay," I said.

She released me, patted me once on the chest, took a deep breath of the evening air and then smiled. "I do love Miami," she said. "I'll always appreciate Brucey bringing me here to retire." She patted me again. "You be good to your mother when she retires," she said.

"She's never worked," I said. "So retiring is more of a state of mind with her."

"She raised you," she said, "and I don't see you out robbing banks. Someone did something right." She went back inside then, apparently content that she'd learned what she needed to know and taught me something, too.

"Spunky lady," Sam said.

I rubbed at my cheeks. "Her fingers were like talons," I said.

"I wouldn't be surprised to find out she did some Bonnie and Clyde business back in the day," Sam said. "Maybe she was Bonnie. We don't know."

"Cops killed Bonnie and Clyde," I said. "We do know."

"A lot of that was covered up," Sam said. "Top secret stuff, Mikey—one day I'll explain it all to you."

There's a line I try not to cross with Sam. Breaking into his delusions was top on the list. So I just moved forward and asked, "How much time does Zadie have left?"

"I don't know," Sam said. "I got what medical reports I could get. They never have the expiration date on them. But not long, Mikey, not long."

"Then we need to make sure she's comfortable," I said.

"And what's the plan to make that happen?"

"I think we need to kill Bruce," I said.

"Novel," he said.

"Actually, first, we use him as bait," I said, "then we kill him."

"And then what, raise him from the dead?"

"Yes," I said.

Sam contemplated my answer. "I don't see how this could fail."

I explained to Sam the framework of the plan. We'd first drive out to one of the Ghouls' clubhouses—the wonderful aspect of dealing with biker gangs is that they actually have clubhouses, which is quaint unless you stumble in looking for a bathroom and end up with a pool cue upside your head—hand them a stack of the documents Bruce took, maybe even some of the vaunted patches, and tell them we have the guy responsible and we're ready to deal. Tell them we caught him breaking into our "business" and that we tortured him and made him talk. And when he talked, he fingered the Banshees, another national gang with a big presence in the lucrative Florida drug trade. They also had a boutique business in prostitution and loan sharking, which made them an all-around great group of guys.

At any rate, the Ghouls would like the torture part. They were big on using welding material and power saws and, apparently, acid.

A normal person driving a Chrysler Sebring would be shot during the course of this action, which is why we were going to play the part. Bikes. Colors. A subservient Fiona to sit behind me. The whole deal. We'd make them an offer on Bruce's head. Get a good sale price to deliver him to them.

"First thing, though," I said, "we need to find Nick Balsalmo's girlfriend. I've got a feeling that if she left him and that apartment just prior to his death, she had to know something was coming."

"You got a name on her?"

"All Bruce knows is that her name is Maria."

"So I need to find a Cuban woman named Maria. That shouldn't be difficult. How many could there be in Miami? Fifty, sixty thousand?"

"I figure you've probably got a buddy who could pull her electric bill," I said.

"Yeah, I could call in a favor or two," he said.

"And I'm going to assume Nick Balsalmo will have a funeral shortly," I said. "He doesn't seem like the kind of guy who had a lot of friends and family, so I'm going to say Maria turns up sooner than later. We get her to finger the Ghouls definitively in Nick's death, we have something to bargain with."

"And if she doesn't do that?"

"Motorcycle gangs in Florida tend to have pretty defined turf and markets," I said. "I'm sure once the Ghouls find out that the local chapter of the Banshees hired Bruce to knock them over, and us, that they'll be ready to kill someone."

Sam started to smile. "I see me wearing a leather vest at some point. You know, not to brag, but there was a time when a man could wear a leather vest and no shirt and make that work. You don't see that too much anymore."

Fiona hopped down from the roof then—literally, she came off the low lip of the roof above the porch and landed as gracefully as a gymnast. "This time you speak of," she said to Sam, as if she'd been in the conversation with us the entire time, "this was when? Antiquity?"

Sam looked up at the roof. "What was that, a twelve-foot drop?"

"I'm very agile," she said.

"You're not wearing any shoes," Sam said.

"And you're talking about wearing a vest and no shirt and making it work. There are mysteries beyond what anyone can perceive, apparently." She turned her gaze to me. "I heard a rumor about me being property. Is that accurate?"

"If you'd like," I said, "I'd be happy to give you a copy of the Ghouls' constitution and you can read it for yourself."

"No need," she said. "I rather like the idea of being subservient to you and then springing into the face of some man with a handlebar mustache and teaching him a thing or two about how to respect a woman."

"That's wonderful news, Fi," I said. "But you know that when these bikers get into a fight, it's never one-on-one. They'll rat-pack you."

"Which is why you and Sam will be there to defend my honor. And why I'll have a very powerful gun—

currently being used to help a rebel cause in Cuba—in my purse."

"I don't think Kate Spade will go with the leather pants and bikini-top ensemble I'm sort of picturing you in there, Fiona," Sam said.

"Is that what I get to wear?" she asked me.

"That's the general uniform," I said.

"Lovely," she said. "I'll bring two guns and a knife. Maybe a blackjack, too, just for fun."

Sam and I both looked at Fi and tried to do the math. It wasn't working. But I'd seen her fight plenty of times, and if she said she was going to carry two guns, a knife, a blackjack and a SCUD missile, I figured she'd put it all somewhere.

"I gotta run, Mikey," Sam said. "I'm meeting my guy with the bikes at the Carlito, and then in the morning I'll see what I can find on Maria. You need anything else?"

I opened the door into the house and listened for screaming. All I heard was the TV. *Wheel of Fortune* was on and someone had just lost everything, which was evident by my mother's loud proclamation "They rig the game, Zadie, that's why," which I could only imagine answered some very important question as to the strategy of spinning a wheel covered in money.

I closed the door. "We need to get Bruce and Zadie and my mother apart as soon as possible," I said.

"Yeah," Sam said, "I thought I saw your mom making eyes at Bruce. Frankly she could do a lot worse.

Though I have to say that whole missing-finger business would be a serious distraction. But that's just me."

"Sam," I said.

"Anyway," Sam said, "the house is safe and this will all seem like a bad dream to everyone really soon. Eventually you'll even start to miss old Bruce, at least until we're all back together for the wedding in the final episode."

"That will be sweet," Fi said.

A series of bad decisions by Bruce had left me, once again, in the middle of something beyond my control. It was a great day to be Michael Westen. No doubt. "Let's see if we can get this taken care of as quickly as possible," I said to both Fi and Sam, "before we have to move everyone into one of your homes."

Not surprisingly, this time they both agreed without question.

8

For Sam Axe, tracking down leads was a rather enjoyable process. He frequently got to do it from home,
which meant pants were optional, or from the bar,
which meant umbrella drinks were optional, or poolside, which meant other people's shirts and pants were
optional as well but umbrella drinks were prevalent.
Occasionally he had to track someone down by foot,
and that was okay in the larger scheme of things, too,
since tracking someone through the streets of Miami
was a far better option than through the dunes of
Kabul.

Still, the one thing he was absolutely certain about
was that if a person feared for their life, they were much
more difficult to actually find. Oh, you could figure out
who they were, but *where* they were was an entirely different set of circumstances.

The easiest way to figure out Maria's full name and
likely whereabouts would be to simply go back to the
apartment where she had lived with Nick Balsalmo and
poke around, maybe see if there was some mail with

her name on it sitting about, talk to the neighbors. But since the news the previous night had been full of grisly reporting about Balsalmo's death, it didn't seem prudent. Homicide cops tend to ask a lot of questions that Sam really had no prepared set of answers for, beginning with the inevitable "What are you doing here?"

And then when Sam picked up the morning's *Miami Herald* and flipped to the local news section and saw that the media had already been through the building and found the inhabitants strangely quiet—no one, it seemed, had heard anyone being brutally murdered, which was odd since Sam could hear his neighbors doing all sorts of things, none of which included dismemberment—he decided that pounding on doors and skulking around might lead to him getting into more trouble than was needed. How hard could it possibly be to find someone named Maria, especially someone with a previous address?

Hard, it turns out, which was why Sam was sitting in the driving test bay at the DMV waiting for his buddy Rod Lott to come out. Of all the people Sam could call on, he really preferred staying away from people in the DMV. They just weren't like normal human beings. Sam chalked it up to dealing with the lowest common denominator of society each and every moment of each and every day.

It's not as if fighting wars for a living was a great way to make new supersmart friends, nor, really, was this current way of life he was leading, where he spent most of his time helping other people out of their problems by, well, fighting miniature wars. But at least the people he worked for had interesting problems, even if they weren't active members of Mensa. Sam had no idea just how many mobsters, drug dealers, crazy gun-toting boyfriends and assassination plots he'd foiled in the last year or so, but his life was different each day, and there was value in that. The night before, after putting tactical razor wire around Madeline's house, he'd met up with an ex-undercover DEA agent who gave him the address of the Ghouls' hangout and hooked him up with two very nice choppers. Not everyone got to do that every day, right?

Sometimes Sam wondered how much longer he could do this running-around blowing-stuff-up business and then he saw people like Rod Lott and knew that he would keep doing it until, well, until the beer was free and paid for entirely by his pension, because when Rod stepped out of the office and into the bright sun of the Miami morning, Sam had to stifle a laugh. Sam had first met Rod back in 1993 at the Navy base on Diego Garcia. Sam was there preparing for a mission that would eventually take him to Bosnia, and Rod was assigned to the base to push paper from one side of his desk to the other. Guys like that, Sam knew, were always up for a little covert activity with the locals. Problem was, Rod turned out to be a good Catholic, didn't drink, didn't smoke, didn't care to go to Sri Lanka to check out the local talent.

But he didn't mind driving. Or looking. So for two months, Sam corrupted the poor fellow as much as he could, though Rod never did break.

That happened a day after Sam left.

Sam tried not to beat himself up about it, figuring, you know, eventually a boy will be a boy. Now, here Rod was, wearing pressed khaki pants, a short-sleeved white dress shirt and a plain red tie. But it was the black horn-rimmed glasses matched up with his ever-present Navy-issue high-and-tight haircut that got Sam thinking Rod must be back on the Book. You'd need to be on *something* to work at the DMV and look like Ward Cleaver and Buddy Holly's love child.

Rod looked carefully in both directions before entering Sam's car, as if maybe he thought he was being filmed. And then Sam looked up and saw the cameras above the doors to the DMV and realized that, in fact, he was.

"Sam," Rod said. His voice was monotone, but then the guy never was much on octave change, but the sad thing was that he also stared straight ahead, unblinking. The DMV had turned the poor kid into a robot.

"How you doing, Big Rod?" Sam said.

Nothing.

Oh, hell, Sam thought, and turned straight forward, too. Whatever game he had to play to protect this job of Rod's, he'd play. "Rod," Sam said.

"Drive," Rod said.

It was going to be difficult to get the information

he needed if Rod spoke only one word at a time, but Sam was under the impression that maybe once they got out of the direct range of the DMV Rod would loosen up.

"You got a direction for me?" Sam asked.

"East," Rod said.

"That left or right here at the street?"

Rod reached into his pocket and pulled out a compass. He was still Navy, that was for sure. You gotta trust a person who carries a compass around. "Right and then your first left," he said.

Ah, finally, more than one word. Progress.

Sam drove and Rod kept giving him directions and Sam kept following them. He noticed that on Rod's lap was an envelope filled with documents. A good sign.

After twenty minutes of meandering around the streets of Miami, Sam was starting to get both frustrated and bored, so when they got to a stoplight he said, "You got a destination in mind, Big Rod?"

"We need to find a vector not commonly used by DMVstaff," he said.

Christ. Anyone who used the word "vector" on a regular basis and wasn't still behind a gun needed help.

Sam looked around the area, tried to reconnect himself with the city a bit, see if he could find a place nearby that might suffice before he strangled the life out of Rod. Kitty-corner to them was a nice-looking bar called the Blue Yonder, which is to say it looked like the kind of place you went right before you skipped town on a warrant.

"You hear about a lot of DMV guys drinking at the Blue Yonder?" Sam asked.

Rod shifted in his seat. Maybe he didn't drink anymore. Sam couldn't imagine how that might be, considering how buttoned-up the guy was. If it was Sam, he'd need a drink just to put that damn tie on. "Fine," Rod said when the light turned green. "But you won't mind if I don't imbibe."

"Roger that," Sam said, just trying to make Rod feel comfortable, and as an experiment, maybe if he simulated the sounds of radio talk, he'd get Rod to respond like a carbon-based life-form. Sam was actually feeling worried. He wasn't sure if Rod was still in this body or if he'd been sucked out by the alien queen.

The parking lot of the Blue Yonder was filled with late-model American cars, always a good sign that the clientele was only in town long enough to cash the check they'd kited, and even still Rod looked cautious getting out. They made their way into the bar and took a seat in a dark booth. Sam made out five guys drinking alone, one woman who might have been a man in drag and, curiously, a civet cat hooked to a chain leash sitting placidly next to the bar. A TV over the bar was tuned to highlights on ESPN, but no one seemed to be watching, except for the bartender, who kept a running conversation with the anchors and, Sam decided, the cat. The other patrons didn't seem to pay any mind to the cat, but whenever something interesting showed up on the television, the bartender would turn to the cat and say a sentence or two.

"That A-Rod is a bum, right, Scooter?" the bartender said. The cat turned at the sound of his name, but didn't have a ready response.

"You know they eat those in China," Rod said, referring to the cat.

"Really?" Sam said. He was just happy Rod was finally communicating.

"They're a delicacy. But after the SARS outbreak, people stopped eating them as much."

"Why is that?" Sam asked.

Rod looked at the cat kind of sideways, which reminded Sam of the way Rod used to look at the women on the streets of the Maldives. "They carried the disease," Rod said.

This really was a dive bar, Sam thought.

"Good to know," Sam said. "One less food I need to worry about being forced to eat."

"They also make coffee out of their fecal matter," Rod said.

"Who are 'they'?"

Rod didn't respond. He was still looking at the cat, though he actually seemed to be trying to do some sort of mind-meld with it. It wasn't unusual for people to leave the military and then join either the post office or the DMV, as both required a slavish, military degree of subservience. Both also required people to find joy in repetition, which was just a precursor to madness as far as Sam was concerned. Doing the same thing every day and expecting to go home happy wasn't the definition of madness, but damned if Sam could figure out why it wasn't, since Rod seemed positively loopy.

"So, Big Rod, the little errand I asked you to do," Sam said, "what do you have for me?"

Rod handed Sam the envelope, but kept his eye on the cat. Whatever was happening there was between Rod and the cat. Sam pulled out the documents and started going over them. According to what Rod had pulled from the computer, the woman living at the address where Nick Balsalmo had met his demise was a seventy-five-year-old woman named Maria Cortes. The DMV had her going five-two and weighing in at 283 pounds. That didn't seem right. Sam had seen stuff on the Internet, of course, but Nick Balsalmo was a thirty-five-year-old guy running drugs out of Little Havana. He didn't seem like a granny chaser.

"Rod, you sure about this?" Sam said.

Rod finally turned his attention from the cat and regarded Sam with something like disappointment. "Of course," he said, as if he couldn't believe he was being questioned.

"See, the thing is, I think I'm looking for someone younger."

"These Cuban families," Rod said and then drifted

off in his sentence, his eye back on the cat. "Is that thing getting closer to us?" he asked.

"No," Sam said. "It's on a chain." He wondered if Rod had suffered some kind of mild stroke. "What were you saying about these Cuban families?"

"Maybe half of them are legal, the other half came on a boat, they all use the same names. Could be twelve Maria Corteses in that family."

That was already something Sam had considered, which meant that the real Maria in question here was probably illegal, which would make it doubly hard to track her down.

"Did you happen to run any old car registrations for this person?"

"It's all there, Sam," Rod said, though he kind of spat the words out. "I took initiative."

Guy sure was bitter, Sam thought, but after pulling through a few pages, he found a current registration for a 1991 Honda Civic to an address only a few miles from the building where Balsalmo was killed. It was a place to start.

He sifted through the rest of the papers and found a few more car registrations, along with a permit for a vehicle not currently being operated dated a few months earlier to the same address as the Civic. A 1977 Ford Ranchero. A good sign.

"What do I owe you for this stuff, Rod?"

"Nothing," Rod said.

"No favor I can do for you?"

"No," Rod said. He'd locked eyes with the civet, which had begun to emit a low growl. "You ever feel like you were born into the wrong species?"

"Can't say that I have," Sam said.

"You know of any available jobs out there in the private sector, Sam?"

"You're in the private sector," Sam said.

"You know what I mean," he said. "Something where I got a little action."

If it was up to Sam, he'd prescribe a course of action for Rod that involved large sums of psychotropic drugs, followed by intensive regression therapy. And a promise that he would never be allowed to proctor a line at the DMV again.

"Can't say that I do," Sam said.

"Then what are you doing? Why do you need this information?"

Sam was pretty comfortable with most of his friends. They rarely asked questions, and when they did it was usually just to protect their own asses. Understandable. But Rod seemed like he just wanted a piece of the action.

"I'm doing some process serving," Sam said. "Maria here is getting sued by Sears. Owes thirteen hundred on a Bowflex she bought on credit. It's actually a pretty interesting case." Sam continued to prattle on until Rod lost interest and started staring at the cat again, which caused the cat to start pacing back and forth on its leash, that low growl turning more guttural. After a good five minutes essentially describing the plot of an episode of *Simon & Simon* that he remembered, Sam concluded by saying, "So, if you're interested in that, just let me know."

By this time, the other patrons in the bar had noticed the cat's change in personality and were scooting to the other side of the bar, which reminded Sam of how people used to sit in the nonsmoking section on airplanes, as if the metal tube they were locked in could somehow discern where the smoke went. If that weird-ass cat thing decided to rip away from the wall and attack Rod and start eating faces, it was Sam's impression that being on the other side of the bar would only increase the fun for the beast. The only person who didn't move was the drag queen—or who Sam had decided was a drag queen, since very few women that he knew had a growth of beard and a tattoo of a naked woman riding a dragon inked on their forearms. It was a good disguise, anyway, and suggested that an aggressive Asian cat was the least of his (her?) concerns.

Unfortunately, the bartender was not so encumbered, as he noticed the change. "Easy, Scooter, easy," he said, and then started to make his way over to the table with a bat in his hand. Sam didn't know what he was planning with the bat, and anyway it was all a little too late, really, since Sam had wanted a beer about fifteen minutes earlier, but now just wanted to get psycho Rod back to the DMV before he did even more damage in public. Sam yanked Rod out of the booth by his sleeve and got him out the door before they had to fight their way out. Used to be you could go into a bar without encountering civet cats and drag queens, but Sam thought maybe it was the person he was hanging out with that brought on these odd circumstances. Sam made a mental note to find a better DMV source, perhaps someone who hadn't been mentally neutered at some point in the recent past.

An hour later, Sam parked in front of a house on the eastern edge of Little Havana. It was an old house, probably built before 1930, conveniently located next to a coin-wash Laundromat and Kwik Stop on Northwest 8th. Across the street was the Olancho Café and a dollar store. It was one of those weird neighborhoods where these classic old houses were now wedged between commercial properties, which for Sam was a good thing. It meant that you could park in front of a house and no one would assume you were casing it, even when that's precisely what you were doing.

The house looked to be no more than a thousand square feet, but there were enough cars parked behind the chain-link fence separating the property from the sidewalk to suggest that those thousand square feet were being occupied by quite a few people. The Honda Civic was there, as was an old Ford truck, its hood a rusted red, a lowered Camaro, a primer-colored Karmann Ghia on blocks and, parked all the way in the back, the Ranchero. It had a camper shell on it, which looked absurd, but then Sam didn't exactly consider the Ranchero a practical car as it was.

From the exterior, the house looked to be in good shape. It had a fresh coat of yellow paint, the front porch was trimmed in white, there was a rocking chair just beside the front door—which was open—and an Adirondack-style chair on the other side. Whoever lived here, Sam thought, actually *lived* here.

The chain-link fence was joined in the center by two swinging gates padlocked together. Sam never understood why people somehow thought padlocks would keep them safe or keep their possessions from being stolen. All anyone needed to do was climb over the fence, hot-wire the car and drive it right through the fence. Or, with two paper clips, they could pop the padlock open in under twenty seconds. Sure, if you shoot a lock it might not open, but if you actually just disengage the locking system, it'll pop right open.

Running around inside the fencing was a big Labrador. Another good sign.

Sam got out of his car and walked up to the fence. He could hear the drone of a television coming from the inside. The television was turned to either the news or an action film, as all he could hear was explosions and screams and sirens. Hard to tell the difference these days. The Labrador was rolling around with a stuffed penguin on the mostly dirt front lawn, paying Sam absolutely no attention in the least. Sam had a brief vision of what it would be like with that weird-ass civet in there, too. The Lab would probably lick it to death.

"Hello?" Sam shouted. He did it a couple more times until an older gentleman wearing Bermuda shorts and no shirt came out onto the front porch.

"What do you want?" he asked.

Real pleasant.

"Chuck Finley," Sam said. "From the Department of Motor Vehicles. "

"You got a warrant?"

"No, sir," Sam said. "Not a criminal matter. Just here about the registration on your Ranchero there in the back."

The man walked down the front steps, stopped next to the dog and just stared at the animal, like he was trying to will it into action. "Some guard dog," the man said. "My stepdaughter, she tells me this dog will help keep us safe. Two years, it's never barked once. I don't even know if it has vocal cords. Just chases that stuffed penguin around the yard all day."

The man knelt down and scratched the dog's head. The man was older, but Sam couldn't figure out just how old. He had ruddy brown skin and his eyes carried deep bags, but his shirtless torso was lean and muscular. No tats, no notable scars, not even really any hair to speak of. He could be fifty. He could be seventy.

"Man's best friend," Sam said. "He'd probably bark if a penguin walked up." The man snorted out a laugh, but didn't move any closer to the gate or make a move to let Sam in. "So, about the Ranchero. I just need to check to make sure you've not been driving it."

"I look stupid to you?" the man said. He looked at Sam without any sense of aggression, maybe because he was still petting his dog. Studies said dogs made people more placid. Maybe they were right. "Since when does the DMV make house calls?"

"Part of the stimulus plan," Sam said. The great thing about the stimulus plan the government had recently put into motion was that no one had any idea what was in it. You could tell people purple monkeys were part of the stimulus plan and if you said it with some conviction, they would consider it for at least a few minutes.

But not this guy.

"If you're looking for my stepdaughter," he said, "she's gone."

Not a good sign.

"Out shopping?"

"How many times do you think you can threaten someone before they get the hint?"

"What about you?"

"I've lived here fifty years," he said. "No one ever comes here and threatens me. She has her own life. I live here too long to be bothered by idiots."

"You the original owner of the house?" Sam said. Just keeping it light. Pretending that bit about the threat slid right past him.

"It was built in 1929. I moved in a few days later," the man said, a hint of a laugh in his voice. Keeping it light, too, but still not budging from his spot next to the dog.

"When did Maria move in?"

"You do think I'm stupid, don't you?"

Not good again. The thing was, Sam got the sense the man was enjoying the game.

"What did you say your name was?" Sam asked.

"Shouldn't you know that?"

Sam walked back to his car and pulled out the envelope of documents. They were all in the name of Maria Cortes.

"I'm looking for a young woman named Maria," Sam said. "Or a big woman named Maria. You're not either of them, right?"

"DMV doesn't know if I'm a man or a woman? I've been driving a car since before you were born."

The problem wasn't with the DMV. It was with all of the government. "Yes, yes," Sam said, "I see it here." He didn't, but that didn't mean he was going to admit that. See if maybe the man would just give up his damn name, make it easy on everyone.

"What did you say *your* name was?"

"Chuck Finley," Sam said.

"Like the ballplayer?"

"No, not like anyone. Just me. Chuck Finley."

"There was another Chuck Finley," he said. "Owned baseball teams."

"That was Charles O. Finley," Sam said. "That's not me, either."

"Could be you," he said. "That guy was known not to play on the level too much. He once tried to trade his manager. Who does that?"

"Not me," Sam said, trying to figure the guy out. It seemed clear he was smart, knew a few things about life and didn't believe a single thing Sam was saying. Sam sort of admired him for that. These old Cuban guys. They'd seen so much crap in their lives, it almost didn't make sense to try to con them for information.

"One other thing you got going for you?" he said. "You're not like the other dudes been showing up. You got a car. Not a nice car, but not some screaming motorcycle."

Uh-oh.

"You said you were Maria's stepfather?"

"That's what I said."

"Her mother around?"

"No," he said. "They left together. Fine by me."

"You're a tender guy," Sam said. He decided being straight was the only way to get what he needed. He wasn't sure it was a two-way street, however. "Bad guys come here looking for your stepdaughter and you just boot her out?"

"She got in with a bad crowd," he said. "I warned her that Nick was no good, and so she came crawling back here, I told her, 'See, I told you.' But she's a grown woman now. Her mother, too. What can I do?"

"Maria is in a lot of trouble," Sam said. "I'm not here to hurt her. I'm here to protect her."

"I bet."

"Her boyfriend Nick is dead."

"I told you he was a bad guy."

"He was cut up in pieces inside an apartment rented in your wife's name," Sam said. "Then he was dumped in acid. Was he that bad? Is anyone that bad?"

The man stopped petting the dog, considered the sentence Sam said, patted the dog once and then stood up. Finally, Sam thought, a reaction.

"You're not with those bikers?"

"No," Sam said.

"And you're not DMV, right?"

"Right."

This answer actually seemed to ease him more than the negative answer on the biker issue. Everyone hates the DMV. No wonder Rod was how he was. "I'm José," he said. "And I drive that Ranchero all the time. Just hate to get it registered, you know? Piece of crap. Let it sit."

"Right," Sam said.

"Now, then, who are you?" José asked.

There was the rub. Sam couldn't quite tell him the truth and couldn't quite lie, not if he wanted his help in getting Maria safe. "I'm just someone who wants to help her stay alive." Sam scratched out his cell phone number on the back of the envelope and reached it over the fence toward José. He finally moved away from the dog and took the envelope. "I don't care if she's illegal. I don't care about anything but keeping her safe."

"She'll call you tonight," José said and then he and the dog went inside, closing the door quietly behind them.

9

Before you attack a fixed enemy position, you always want to do a proper amount of reconnaissance. This is true if you intend to attack with firepower or if you intend to attack with psychological warfare. Either option requires a precise understanding of the lay of the land.

The first order of business is to obtain as much information about the physical area as possible. This is usually done by having several different people watching the same area from different vantage points, who then obtain salient intelligence and report back. In an ideal situation, all of that intel would be gathered and then you'd grid out the area from all angles and plan your attack.

You'd then break into seven teams: the assault team, which does the assaulting; the security team, which handles securing the area from reinforcements; the support team, which assists the assault team indirectly; the breach team, which cuts through obstacles; the demolition team, which blows stuff up; and the search team, which is sent to ferret out any remaining hostiles.

To do this effectively, a team of about fifty men would be best. A dozen claymore mines would help, some tank support wouldn't offend anyone and an extraction team with a gassed-up Black Hawk would make it a nice, polite party

If you have less than fifty men, no claymores, no tanks and only a DVD of *Black Hawk Down*, you're going to need to make adjustments. When you're a spy, you're often asked to do the work of fifty men simply by being better at everything.

Being better doesn't really matter when a dozen violent bikers are beating you to death with lead pipes because you've cornered yourself due to poor planning, which is why Fiona and I were down the street from the Ghouls' clubhouse just west of the airport watching who was coming and who was going, and attempting to figure out what the odds were that we could bust in and start making outlandish demands. I was keeping watch with binoculars and a camera with a telephoto lens. Fiona was keeping watch by reading *InStyle* magazine and periodically taking cell phone calls

"Why are the police able to pester Britney Spears and Lindsay Lohan every ten minutes but can't arrest these men at their own clubhouse?" Fiona asked.

"Because they aren't doing anything wrong," I said. It was true: Their clubhouse was technically a bar and they were technically patrons, which is perfectly legal. And since you could refuse service to anyone as a shop owner, they didn't have a problem with not serving a person who might wander in off the street. Though the monster sitting in front of the door absently twirling a baseball bat probably dissuaded most casual onlookers. In the last hour, we'd watched about a dozen men who looked essentially just like Baseball Bat roll up on their bikes and enter the bar. Usually these guys had a few women with them—you could tell who they were since they wore jackets that said PROPERTY OF THE GHOULS on the back, because the Ghouls aren't exactly known for their grand subtlety—but not today. It had been been a bad week for the company and it looked like they were doing some official business. Trying to place a legal bug into what is ostensibly a public place is a significant legal issue, which made the Ghouls' use of a de facto clubhouse right out in the open a pretty savvy bit of criminality.

"This article says Britney is an excellent mother," Fi said.

"I don't think anyone thinks these guys are excellent mothers," I said. "It's going to be a challenge getting to the front door without hurting someone."

That got Fi's attention, so I handed her the binoculars. "That's a cute bat he has," she said. "Looks like he also has a cute gun under his gut."

"I saw that, too."

"If you're that fat," Fi said, "isn't it hard to ride a motorcycle?"

"Maybe he just stands around looking tough," I said. That was part of the Ghouls' game: Scare the crap out of you just by looking frightening. Baseball Bat fit that description. He was over six feet tall, had long, shaggy hair that reached past his shoulders, a handlebar mustache, a classy tattoo on his throat of a gun barrel pointed into his chin, which was sort of imposing until you considered that it probably just meant he was suicidal or incredibly stupid. Probably both. He also ran at least three bills. Maybe three-fifty.

"How long would it take for you to take him down?" I asked.

"I could do it right now," she said. "I'd just walk by with a bag of donuts and some crystal meth and he'd follow me like a dog."

"I mean if push came to shove and Sam and I were fighting the other ten guys."

Fiona focused the binoculars. "I could have him down in ten seconds. One punch to the throat. Maybe a kick to the knee first. He must be in terrible knee pain holding up all that weight." She handed me the binoculars and went back to reading her magazine.

"That's my girl," I said.

"And if neither of those moves worked, I'd just shoot him."

A gold Lincoln Continental pulled up in front of the clubhouse—which was actually a bar called Purgatory, which made it about as inconspicuous as the Baseball Bat out front—and three men got out, two from the front seat, one from the back. The man from the back-seat was huge, too, but wore a suit, nice shoes, a big watch, like he was a pit boss in Las Vegas. The two other men wore jeans and boots, had long hair, handlebar mustaches and lots of neck ink.

"What do we have here?" I said.

Fi looked up from her magazine but didn't bother taking the binoculars. "Do Lincolns come stock in gold?"

"Not usually," I said. I set down the binoculars and picked up the camera and took a couple of pictures through the zoom lens.

Baseball Bat greeted the man in the suit with a fist pump, the other two men the same way, and let them into the clubhouse and then quickly closed the door. He took several steps down the street and looked around, though not very well. He didn't bother to notice me and Fi in the Charger less than a block away. But then, maybe the people he was worried about weren't the kind to sit in a car a block away with binoculars.

Baseball Bat moseyed back to his post, which took him some time and effort. Fi was right: Kicking him in the knee would probably take him out of commission for the foreseeable future.

Motorcycle gangs have tried to diversify their business practices. The Hells Angels have a very popular fund-raiser for sick kids, for instance, and sell stickers and buttons and T-shirts. The Outlaws have tattoo parlors where sorority girls get dolphins inked onto their hips. The Ghouls, however, were trying to keep it real by selling drugs and hurting people for fun and profit, but the appearance of the man in the Lincoln had me interested. Clearly he was of some serious importance, because no one else driving a gold Lincoln would be treated as well by old Baseball Bat. And also the man in the Lincoln was the last person to arrive. All of the other bikers got there plenty early.

Real power is the ability to arrive late and without an excuse while knowing that not a single person will question you. If you want to prove to yourself just how important you are, waste other people's time.

I reached into the backseat and grabbed the Ghouls' constitution and flipped to the section on leadership structure. The odd thing about the Ghouls' constitution was that it was actually quite well constructed, even in how it meted out payments on drug sales, shylock business and prostitution and a nebulous other category called "incidental accruing accounts," which I suppose could mean just about anything from stealing wallets to knocking over a Brinks truck. It made sense, really, since the first members of the Ghouls were ex-military coming back from Vietnam, guys who lived by a code and were shit on for it and came back with drug problems and a desire to flip off the government they worked for.

And it looked like they'd succeeded. Not that any of the current members were likely ex–Delta Force, but the militaristic formation of the group added layers of bureaucracy to their business dealings, which meant you needed one guy who wasn't always driving around on a chopper to make decisions and order punitive damages.

A guy in a gold Lincoln, for instance.

"I'm going to say the gentleman in the bad suit and pinkie ring is the local president," I said. There was also a vice president, a recording secretary, a sergeant-at-arms and even a road captain, who was in charge of booking hotel reservations and such when they went on long rides. Sort of sweet, really, like a cruise director who will beat you to death for looking at him wrong.

"What kind of man becomes the president of a motorcycle gang and then consents to drive that car?"

It was a good question.

"Why don't you go find out?"

"Really?"

"Really. Why don't you go see if you can use the restroom in Purgatory. See what they're talking about. If you can't hear them, leave some ears behind."

Fi closed her magazine, leaned over and kissed me on the cheek. "The day is not a total waste," she said.

She reached into the backseat and started rummaging through her purse, dumping out various weapons. She probably wanted to travel light.

When you're planning an assault, occasionally the best use of intelligence is to throw it all out the window and send in your best person to shoot the man in charge in the head.

That's usually been my job.

When you have a weapon like Fiona, who looks as

if she'd blow away in a brisk breeze but who relishes violence like most women covet new shoes, you have to learn to use her wisely. Sending her into the Ghouls' clubhouse would assure two things:

That when I went back the next day, I'd know all the avenues of escape, precisely what might be used as a weapon and all of the soft spots in the men.

That when I went back the next day with Fiona by my side, they'd know I already had the upper hand, that they'd been gamed, and, maybe, they'd start wondering if someone in their midst was talking to the wrong people.

All of that was working on the assumption that Fiona didn't end up permanently disfiguring anyone.

I took her by the wrist. "Take as many guns as you like," I said, "but please try not to kill anyone. It won't help Bruce in the least."

"I will try not to kill anyone. Kneecapping is allowed if need be, correct?"

"Correct."

"If I'm not out in ten minutes," she said, "please come and get me."

"If you're not out in ten minutes," I said, "I'll already be inside."

"That's sweet," she said.

"Be careful."

"Michael, I must say that I like this new sensitivity. Where did you learn it?"

"Something I'm trying out," I said.

"It doesn't really suit you," she said.

"I know."

"But keep trying, will you?"

She popped out of the car then and began sashaying up the sidewalk toward the bar.

The Ghouls didn't stand a chance.

10

When you're hot, you don't need to know a bunch of spy tricks to get information. Men, women, small children and the occasional pet all tend to respond to a pretty girl. This made being Fiona a rather pleasurable experience. She didn't like to think that things had been handed to her on a silver platter simply because she was attractive—and really, if you're going to have something on a platter, would it be a life of crime? No, Fiona tended to believe that she was given good looks to combat the other, less desirable aspects of her personality.

Like the tendency she'd had since childhood to punch people in the neck when they bothered her. Or her general desire to watch things blow up. And then there was her attraction to unavailable men, who, if they had even a smidgen more moral turpitude than she did, would turn her in for what were likely hefty rewards offered on her worldwide. You sell guns to revolutionaries and just common scumbags and people tend to take it the wrong way, but that was okay by Fiona.

A girl has to earn a living. Particularly if she doesn't

want to depend on a man for a living. That was the one thing she just couldn't resolve in her mind as she walked up to Purgatory. How could women consent to being the property of not just one drug-dealing biker but an entire gang? Oh, maybe a certain brand of woman found that exciting for a few days, but eventually didn't you wake up in bed next to the sweating beast and realize you were being treated worse than a whore? Didn't that bother those women? *InStyle* tended not to cover that side of life, but Fiona wondered if maybe Oprah could talk some sense into those women. Or maybe that nice Michelle Obama. Now there was a person Fiona thought could handle herself in any situation.

If there was one thing Fiona was certain of, it was that she could handle herself and if you got in her way, well, she'd step right over you. After knocking you down, of course.

She was only a few yards from Purgatory and was overwhelmed by the smell of urine coming from an alley between the bar and the empty shop she was passing. It was odd. All of the stores in this strip of shops were vacant, even though they faced a busy intersection. But then biker piss had a way of driving away business.

The presence of Baseball Bat probably wasn't helping commerce, either. Fiona could see his shadow on the sidewalk, and even that was huge. She also had the sneaking suspicion that some of that smell was coming off him. Nevertheless, when she skipped past the alley and found herself in front of the bar (which was rather daintily designed out front, with a low retaining wall lined with big decorative planters), she gave Baseball Bat a smile that could have melted lead.

"Well, hello to you," she said and that big, scary-looking thug actually blushed.

This was going to be fun.

"Hello to you," he said. His voice was surprisingly sweet-sounding. Somewhere under all of that menace was a boy, Fiona thought. Not much of a boy was left, granted, and probably what was left was a boy who liked to kill animals and melt things, but a boy no less. On his left hand, across the knuckles, was the name CLETE. On his right hand, over his fingers, were the words WILL KILL YOU.

Subtle.

"That's a nice bat," Fi said.

"It gets the job done."

"Cricket?"

"Not quite. You lost, sweetheart?"

"My car broke down," she said. She pointed back toward the Charger, but there were several beaters parked on the street near it and Fiona didn't think Baseball Bat's vision was that great. She could see that even though he had that rather foul-looking tattoo on his neck he also had the darkened rings around his neck that indicated diabetes. Poor bastard, Fi thought. Too tough to get his blood sugar looked at. No wonder he limped around. He probably didn't have any feeling beneath his knees. "And wouldn't you know I have to use the powder room, too? Isn't that how it always is? Just one problem after another."

Fiona started to make her way toward the bar's door and Clete lifted the tip of his bat off the ground and tapped it on Fi's shin. Not hard. Just enough to stop her momentum. "No ladies' room inside," Clete said. Ah, there was the gruff voice.

"I don't need to have a pretty place to sit," she said, moving forward again. "A little boys' room will be fine."

And there was that bat again. This time two taps on her shin. Not a very polite way to treat a lady having a bad day.

"Use the alley," he said

Fiona admired Clete's code. She really did. He had a job to do and he wasn't going to be swayed by a pretty woman with a small bladder and a broken-down car.

"Are you sure?" Fiona said. She stepped closer to him this time, let him get a whiff of her scent, let him really see her up close.

"Beat it, skank," he said and this time brought the bat down onto her foot. Not hard enough to break anything, nor even cause much pain, but with the clear intent to show Fiona that he could, and would, break her foot if she didn't vacate the premises. Even less polite than poking her in the shins, really. In Fiona's opinion, he'd shown a gross lack of chivalry with her when all she needed to do was use the restroom of the establishment.

Or, well, she believed that if she'd actually been someone in that actual position, his lack of chivalry would have been gross. As it was, calling her a skank was not the right thing to do, no matter the situation.

Fiona kicked the barrel of the bat from the top of her right foot, sending it out of Clete's hand and straight into the air. She caught it in midair with her right hand and in the same motion brought it down across Clete's right knee. As he tumbled forward, she grabbed him by the back of his collar and tossed him down the three short steps in front of Purgatory.

He landed with a dull-sounding thud and Fiona could already tell that she'd fairly ruined his knee, because people's legs really aren't supposed to bend inward, are they? It also seemed like the fall had caused him to break his left wrist and nose, since his face was bleeding profusely and his wrist was bent at a nauseating angle.

She'd done a nice amount of damage to his knee, but Fiona reasoned that other injuries were Clete's own fault. His mass multiplied by the acceleration of his fall did the real work. If he'd bothered to take care of himself, he would only have a broken knee now. Alas, people just didn't take care of themselves as well anymore. Fiona thought that was a personal choice that said legions about a person's self-confidence.

Despite all of this, Clete was trying to get up to go

after Fiona, but was clearly having a pretty hard time of it.

Fiona walked gingerly down the steps—after seeing how Clete took them, she was sure she'd didn't want to slip and land on him, even though with her weight, she'd probably bounce harmlessly off—and stood a few feet from Clete.

"It's not polite to call a girl a skank," she said.

"I'll kill you," Clete managed, but there wasn't much in the way of honest-to-goodness malice in his voice, seeing as he was choking back tears. It's hard to sound really tough when a girl has busted out your kneecap and tossed you to the pavement, though Fiona admired him for trying.

Then she remembered that gun she'd noticed in his belt earlier. Unfortunately for Clete, she remembered it at the very moment he remembered it, too. So as he tried to extract it from beneath his sizable girth, she brought the bat down into the small of his back. Not hard enough to separate his spine, or paralyze him, but certainly hard enough to shatter his tailbone.

Fiona had been taught early on in her life that if you really want to disable someone, you need not run the risk of killing them as well. Breaking someone's tailbone isn't a pleasant experience for anyone, especially since if you do it the right way, it will temporarily make the person feel paralyzed, and if you do it the wrong way, it will make the person think they're paralyzed *and* knock them out.

So Fiona made sure she did it the wrong way, and then, when it was clear that Clete would not be getting up in the near future, she reached into his pants and removed his gun. It was by far the most disgusting thing she'd done all day. Fiona didn't understand how someone could have that much hair coming up out of their pants. Quite vile.

But the gun was nice. A Star Model D .380. Beautiful finger grooves. Platinum plated. A perfect all-purpose killing machine. She slipped it into her purse and then took another look at Clete. She almost felt bad for him, splayed out there on the sidewalk as he was, until she realized she needed to move him, lest someone notice the enormous biker beached in front of Purgatory. Or at least she needed to hide him. She tried to pull him by his leg, but he was just too damn heavy and the dragging would simply take too long. She opted instead to tip him over against the low retaining wall in front of the bar and then drag a few of the handsome planters around him so that he was effectively boxed in from view.

Then she checked her appearance in the window of one of the vacant shops and fairly skipped into Purgatory.

One thing Fiona could never abide in men was their tendency to turn into pack animals when left to their own devices. The result of this tendency was that everywhere they huddled looked the same: brown.

Brown furniture. Brown carpet. Brown walls. Brown television. Brown food. Brown drinks. Brown dirt under their nails. Brown jeans that were once blue. Women were far more interesting, at least in terms of their palettes.

The really weird thing, though, was that places even *smelled* brown when there was an excess of unfettered men about. Scientists would probably call this pheromones or something, but Fiona thought it all boiled down to the fact that men have never learned how to bathe correctly because none of them are willing to change a lightbulb.

This was abundantly clear when she walked into Purgatory and was met with a wall of blackness. It took her eyes several seconds to adjust before she could make out the dark brown bar, the five dark brown stools that sat empty in front of the bar and the skinny man wearing a brown shirt and pointing a brown sawed-off shotgun at her.

"Whoa," Fiona said. Not because she was frightened, but because she figured that someone encountering a shotgun for the first time would be frightened.

"How'd you get in here?" Skinny said.

"Clete said I could use the bathroom," Fiona said.

Skinny relaxed a bit, but not to the point that he lowered his gun. "You his?" he asked.

"I'm nobody's," Fiona said. "But I could be." She kept her eyes on Skinny, but she was also making note of the items in her periphery. There was a door to the right of the bar that looked to head to a small kitchen area. On her left was an EXIT sign above a hallway. She could hear voices coming from that direction.

Smart. They probably had a boardroom where they conducted business, though Fiona mostly imagined a dozen grimy men sitting around a brown table, each of them emitting brown dirt from their pores.

"You shouldn't be in here," Skinny said. "It'll be his ass and mine."

"I just gotta go real quick. No one will even know I was here. And then maybe you and me and Clete can party. He said he was cool if you were cool."

This got Skinny's attention.

Men.

They'd risk getting killed if they thought it might end up that they got themselves a wild time in the process.

"Okay," Skinny said. "Okay." He still had the gun on her, but it felt less like he was doing it because he thought he'd need to shoot her and more like he was doing it because he wasn't much of a multitasker. He needed to think and that couldn't be done while simultaneously moving his arms. "Okay," he said again. He blinked, then set the shotgun down on the bar. It must be nice to be so simple, Fiona thought. How little time would be wasted on things like making choices. "Go on ahead down the hall. Second door on your right. Just don't make no noise. It'll be my ass."

"Oh, it'll be your ass," Fiona said, because she

thought even the broadest innuendo would send poor Skinny into a frenzy of mental activity and that would keep him from walking outside to check on Clete. But just to be sure, she added, "We could party first, without Clete. What's there in the back?"

"The kitchen," he said.

"Is there a flat surface?"

"There's two," he said. "The floor and the counter. Both are pretty dirty." He wasn't acting much like a biker. No bravado. No hubris. No secondary male characteristics, really, apart from that shotgun. Ah, Fiona thought, the front. The reason the bar isn't bugged.

"Why don't you clean up one of them," Fiona said, "and I'll be out in two shakes of a lamb's tail?"

Skinny considered this offer for a moment before coming to a decision. "All right," he said, "but I only got five minutes, so get back out fast."

A true romantic.

Fiona didn't bother to respond; she just batted her eyelashes a bit, mostly in astonishment, and then headed toward the bathroom. Skinny bounded out from behind the bar and into the kitchen and immediately started whistling a tune Fiona recognized as a child's nursery rhyme, though she wasn't sure which one. Maybe "The Farmer in the Dell."

Once she was in the dark hallway, she could clearly make out the loud conversation going on behind the first door on the right. She could stand right outside the door, but that might be a bit too risky. But since the entire bar was made of fiberboard—brown fiberboard, specifically—she had a pretty good idea that being inside the bathroom would be the equivalent of sitting at the same table as the assembled brain trust of the Ghouls Motorcycle Club.

She opened the second door, turned on the light and realized that, in fact, Clete wasn't lying: They didn't have a proper ladies' room. Instead, what she found was a single toilet, a spartan sink and a mirror that was covered in handprints. On the floor were strewn condom wrappers, broken compacts, crushed beer cans and ants. Above the toilet, in a handsome scrawl, were the words PROPERTY OF THE GHOULS. Fiona ached for irony, but was sure there was none to be found.

She decided she just wouldn't touch anything.

Hearing wasn't going to be a problem, but staying invisible might. There were literally a dozen peepholes drilled into the walls of the bathroom so that the idiots in the next room could watch the girls squatting. There were so many that calling them "peepholes" seemed superfluous. There'd be more privacy if the toilet were out in the hall.

Fiona quickly turned the dim overhead light off again and the darkened bathroom filled with crisscrossing pinholes of light from the room next door. She stood in the middle of the room and listened to the conversation. They were going over the details of the break-in and what they'd learned thus far—all things that Fiona already knew, namely that the stolen drugs had been given to Nick Balsalmo and that they'd "taken care of that."

"Do you have a fucking name yet on the crook?" a man said. His voice sounded like sandpaper. Fiona tried to imagine him driving a gold Lincoln.

"All I got is a last name from Nicky," another man said. There was a pause in the room and it sounded like someone was shuffling papers. "Grossman," he said.

"You know how many Grossmans there are in Miami?" Sandpaper said.

"Not too many who've done time," the other said. "Nicky was with him at Glades. He gave us a bunch of different first names, but none of them worked. And now he's not talking."

A laugh erupted and the man with the sandpaper voice said, "Everyone shut up. You think this is funny? This bastard has our shit. All of it. All of you gonna be laughing in prison? You know how hard I've worked to keep your asses on the street? You screw up, you go like those two last night. You want that? Keep laughing. Find this fucker's first name. Find his family. Find everything about him and get me our shit back!"

Fiona decided right then that staying around any longer would be fruitless and dangerous. She'd been gone only a few minutes, so Skinny would be ready for action and probably wouldn't notice her leaving. She reached into her purse and pulled out a cell phone, dialed an eVoice Mail box number she had that delivered a digital voice file directly to an e-mail address, and then wedged the phone between the toilet and the Swiss cheese wall.

The recording wouldn't be admissible in a court of law, but Fiona didn't mind that. If they needed to give it to the police, she was sure they'd figure out a use for it. How she could have used this simple bit of technology when she was a teenager . . .

Fiona stepped out of the bathroom at the same time a squat man with a major-league—and, like everything else in the bar, brown and greasy—mullet came out of the meeting. She thought he looked like a hobbit with a handlebar mustache, really. Sadly, he wasn't looking in Fiona's direction, which was really too bad for him, since Fiona was able to grab the back of his hair and slam his head into the wall, dropping him to the floor in a heap.

Generally, Fiona wasn't big on saying menacing things to passed-out people—what was the use?—but as she stepped over the hobbit and made her way to the front door, she said, "That was for the peepholes."

She paused once to check on Skinny. He'd left the door to the kitchen open, so she could see his shirtless form sweeping up the floor. His class knew no bounds. He'd left his shotgun on the bar, so Fiona picked that up, too. Along with Clete's .380, she'd made a nice profit from this endeavor and also got to beat the crap out of two members of that fine underclass known as biker scum.

A good day.

II

If you get a job working for the CIA directly out of college, you'll most likely spend the duration of your career sitting behind a government-issued metal desk reading mundane government-issued reports on agricultural concerns in Yemen. You'll work from nine to five. You'll have excellent health benefits.

You'll earn slightly less than people in the private sector. You won't get a gun.

You might travel overseas, but most likely you won't.

You won't be asked to kill anyone.

You won't be asked to impersonate anyone.

You won't be asked to do anything, usually. Most of the time, you'll just show up to your office and there will be a stack of papers waiting for you that you certainly didn't ask to receive.

This will be your life.

If you want to travel the world covertly gathering information for the government, the best thing to do is go to college and then join the military, show your superiors a certain aptitude with intelligence and then, one day, you might just get a phone call from an agency that doesn't exist in any formal government books asking you to leave behind the camouflage for a nice suit and a pair of sunglasses.

And even then you probably won't get a gun.

You'll be an analyst or an interrogator or you'll be in charge of analysts and interrogators.

If you want the gun and the charge to use it (or any other weapon, including your own hands) regardless of the Geneva Conventions, it's important to have a slippery moral center that the government views as potentially beneficial. Spreading democracy is the end goal, of course, but it's nice if you're willing to achieve that goal by using any means necessary.

When you're no longer a spy—or waiting to become one again, presuming at some point the axis that tilts your world finally rights itself and the people who've burned you are willing to rescind the lies they've told about you—that slippery moral center (and understanding that you could be doing paperwork in a basement, too, if not for something as random as luck, or chance, or unique dexterity with a firearm) really only comes in handy if you spend your free time with someone like Fiona Glenanne, helping bank robbers with their problems.

"So," I said, "just so we're clear. You kneecapped Clete, cracked his coccyx and broke his wrist all in under ten seconds?"

"It's about being graceful," Fiona said.

"You didn't think that was excessive?"

"Excessive? No. He called me a skank, Michael," she said. "He's lucky to be respirating."

We were parked in front of a medical center in Coconut Grove waiting for Nate to come out with Bruce and Zadie. After hearing the general thrust of the conversation the Ghouls were having—that they were only one step behind Bruce Grossman and it was a short one—I figured providing security on top of Nate's certainly excellent, totally coherent bodyguarding was wise counsel.

"And how long to dispose of the man in the hall? What did you call him?"

"The Hobbit was less than five seconds. One motion and then to the ground he went."

"Less than five seconds, really?"

"It happened so quickly it couldn't even really be measured in time," Fiona said.

The medical plaza teemed with activity, but thus far no one who looked like they manufactured crystal meth for fun and profit. Most likely, those people were trying to figure out how one tiny woman was able to get by three different men without a peep being made. There was a good chance that at least Clete would claim there was more than one person involved, as his pride was likely so high that admitting the truth was worse than the pain of the truth itself.

That is, if they didn't kill him for letting someone in.

The phone recorded fifteen minutes of conversation, ending with the sounds of a person picking up the phone and slamming it into something, most likely the toilet. Maybe the wall, but certainly something solid enough to destroy it.

If they were smart, they would have checked to see the last number dialed by the phone and then maybe they'd try to get that traced and then maybe they'd show up at a server somewhere in Lawrence, Kansas, or wherever eVoice was based. And maybe, if they were really smart, smarter than I or anyone might justifiably give them credit for, they'd muscle out the e-mail address where the recorded messages were sent, which would be good investigative work indeed, except that e-mail address doesn't exist anymore.

Plus, judging from the recording, the phone was destroyed.

There's a reason some people are in biker gangs and some people are spies.

"How long do you think it will take them to find Bruce's name?" Fiona asked.

"Not long," I said. The truth was that all they had to do was go to the Florida Department of Corrections Web site and type in the last name "Grossman" and work their way through the list of released inmates, something I did about five minutes after Fiona delivered her news.

It was a short list.

Only twelve men with the last name Grossman had

been released from Florida prisons in the previous ten years. There were only five men named Grossman actually doing time.

If the Ghouls tended toward the alphabetically inclined, they'd hit Bruce Grossman second on the list of released inmates, right after Abe Grossman. Abe was seventy-seven at the time of his release nine years ago, he'd been incarcerated for twenty-five years and would now be eighty-six.

If they were methodical, maybe they'd look at each person's sentence and crime and decide who would be the likely candidate to rob their stash house. Abe and Bruce seemed least likely, since at sixty-five Bruce probably seemed just as dangerous as old Abe. So maybe they'd try out Kelly Grossman, a twenty-eight-year-old who did time for assault. Or Pierce Grossman, aka Thomas Pierce, aka Pat Gross, forty-three, and released after six years on a fraud charge.

It didn't matter how they conducted their business, really. After what went down that afternoon, the Ghouls would hit Bruce's house soon.

Maybe that night.

The advantage working in Bruce's favor was that he was living at his mother's. It would take the Ghouls more time to locate that record, since it wasn't public. But that's the nice thing about having leverage against common workaday civilians—like, say, the knowledge that they've purchased illegal drugs—if you need information, there is a good chance someone you know can supply it.

That might buy us ten hours. No more than twenty-four.

There was a lifetime of information inside Zadie's house, which meant we needed to change our plan.

I called Sam. "We're going to need those bikes tonight," I said.

"No problem," Sam said. "My guy delivered them both to your place today. Let me tell you, Mike. You've not lived until you've taken one of these choppers through South Beach. Now, I get my fair share of ladies looking my way, there's no question about that, but it's a whole different level of attraction when you've got all that horsepower between your legs."

"That's great, Sam."

"You ever see *Easy Rider*?"

"Once or twice," I said.

"Different time, different place, that could have been us, Mikey, just taking the trails, the lone road, all that. You and me, Mikey, heading to Florida, looking for America."

"Didn't everyone die at the end of that movie, Sam?"

"Well, I'd get a rewrite on that part," Sam said. "I'm just saying, the wind in your hair, smell of coconut oil, ladies in bikinis hopping on the back for rides. It's a little addictive, Mikey."

"That's just great," I said. "What did you learn about Maria?"

Sam told me about his experience with José and the dog. "She hasn't called yet," he said. "But her old man, he wasn't the kind that seemed to scare easy, so I'm going to guess that he probably sent his daughter away. Or his stepdaughter. Whatever she is. Maybe she isn't even family. Who knows? He might have played tough with me, but I can't see him just letting her run off."

"She calls you," I said, "you need to lean on her to come in, get her to Ma's house. That's one more person who knows Bruce, that's one more person who could be dead by tomorrow. These guys don't play around."

"Got it," Sam said.

"And I need you to call your friend at the DMV again," I said. "I need to know who owns this car." I gave him the license number of the gold Lincoln.

"Yeah," Sam said, "about that friend. He's gone rogue. I might need to get this from someone else."

"Get it from Captain Crunch," I said, "it doesn't matter to me. Then let's meet at Grossman's in an hour. We'll need to see about finding some clothes appropriate for a mission."

"Body armor?"

"More like a vest with a nice logo on it, something that says 'dangerous biker gang member.'"

"I'm ahead of you," Sam said. "My guy gave me a nice stash of vests to choose from."

"Who is this guy?"

"Top secret."

"They're all top secret, Sam."

"You ever see *Billy Jack*?"

"Once or twice."

"He's like that guy. Deep cover, though. He said they still use his cover method as a teaching tool in the Czech Republic to this day."

I saw Bruce and Zadie walk out of the medical center, but didn't see my brother, Nate. That wasn't good. "Gotta go," I told Sam and hung up.

"Where's Nate?" I asked Fiona.

"Isn't it good you can't see him? Wouldn't that mean he's doing his job?"

"He's not that talented," I said.

I got out of the car and started cutting through the parking lot. Even though I didn't see anything dangerous, that didn't mean there wasn't something nearby. We were parked a good hundred yards from the entrance to the medical facility, close enough that I could see everything, far enough that Zadie wouldn't see us and freak out. Keeping her sane and feeling safe was job one.

But now they were standing in the wide open—an easy shot for anyone. This wasn't exactly a biker haven—the medical center where Zadie went for her radiation was just a block from CocoWalk, the make-believe downtown of Coconut Grove, so most of the people on the adjacent streets had that vacant zombie-look of people who just want some Hooters wings or a slice of fifteen thousand-calorie Cheesecake Factory cheesecake. But in the last decade, biker gangs in Miami haven't been shy about fighting right out in the open. It's sort of their thing—what would you do if you saw fifteen men with bats smacking the crap out of someone?

If you were smart, you'd not intervene.

At that moment, I didn't see anyone with bats, but I wanted to make sure that if they showed up Bruce and Zadie would be safe.

The only issue is that a parking lot in front of a medical center in Coconut Grove is more dangerous than a minefield.

I dodged a Cadillac driven by a hundred-year-old woman that was backing up whether or not anyone was behind it and a Land Rover driven by a 120-year-old man who couldn't see above the wheel and didn't seem to mind. A Mercedes with a handicap placard nearly ran me over from the side, perhaps because the car's windows were tinted black, to the point that you'd need a flashlight just to find your seat belt.

All that and I still managed to keep my eyes on Bruce and Zadie.

Where was Nate?

A black Lincoln Town Car skidded to a stop in front of me, ten yards or so from the front of the medical plaza. Just as I was about to reach for my gun, the window rolled down.

"Easy there, big shot," Nate said. "This isn't a pedestrian state."

"Actually," I said, "it is. And this pedestrian almost shot you in the face. Where have you been?"

"I wasn't going to just sit here in the parking lot," Nate said. "What if someone made me?"

"What if?" I said. Nate didn't have an answer. He got out of the car and walked over to Bruce and together they helped Zadie across the short path of the parking lot. Her face was flushed red and she was sweating.

"How are you?" I asked her.

"Nuclear," she said and then got into the backseat without saying another word.

"She's always pretty fired up after radiation," Bruce said. "She's both wired and tired at the same time. It's a terrible way to be."

"I'm sorry," I said.

There was a sad look on Bruce's face. I had to imagine that none of this was what he wanted from this life. But we make choices and we deal with the ramifications. His mother's illness was beyond his control; everything else he'd done belonged to him. "I guess we all get old," he said finally.

"That's the hope," I said, though I wasn't convinced that Bruce was going to get to be as old as his mother. He'd pissed off the wrong people.

"Where's that Fiona?" he asked, his demeanor brightening noticeably.

"She's sitting in a car about a hundred yards from here," I said. "She's probably got a gun pointed at you, but don't take it personally."

"I don't," he said. "May I ask you a personal question?"

"No," I said.

He ignored me. "Is she your . . . uh . . . girlfriend? Is that the right word?"

"Yes," said Nate.

"No," I said.

"So, if it's no," Bruce said, "do you think I could, if everything works out here with us, ask her out?"

"No," I said.

"No," Nate said.

At last, we agreed on something.

Bruce shrugged. "I thought I'd ask," he said.

"Get in the car, Bruce," I said.

Bruce opened his mouth to say something, thought better of it and then walked around to the other side of the car and got into the front passenger seat.

"Interesting guy," Nate said.

"That's not the word I'd use," I said.

"Last night? After you guys went to sleep, we sat up telling war stories. You know he robbed something like a hundred banks?"

"That's what he says," I said.

"Never once used a gun. Never even hurt anyone."

"That's what he told you?"

"He even had a nickname. You wanna hear it?"

"The Idiot?" I said.

"The Gray Grifter," Nate said.

"Fiona said he was called the Safe-Deposit Bandit," I said.

"That's not much of a nickname," Nate said.

"No," I said. "And he wasn't gray when he was robbing all of those banks."

"No?"

"No," I said. "A hundred banks. Really?"

"He said he didn't have an exact number. Anything more than three or four is nails."

"Right," I said. "Nails."

"Way he explained it," Nate said, "he ended up only keeping the stuff he needed. Gave back most of it. Only stole from people he thought could really afford it. That seems okay to me in the long run."

It was time to give Nate an object lesson. "Where'd you get this car?"

"It's a rental," he said. I didn't believe him. But that was an issue for another day.

"So if I saw you on the street," I said, "it would appear you'd have enough money to weather the loss of whatever you might keep in your safe-deposit box, right?"

"Well . . ."

"Precisely," I said.

"He said he'd show me some tricks."

"And Dad and Mom once vowed to love each other through sickness and health," I said. "Not everything is as it seems."

Nate sucked on his bottom lip for a second. I always had to remind myself not to be so hard on Nate, but the problem was that he was like a dog who never learned to stop peeing on the rug. You loved the dog, but, man, you got sick of cleaning up after it made a mess.

"Listen," I said, "things are heating up. I need you to get Bruce and Zadie back to Ma's, but I want you to go a different route than the one you took here."

"How many routes are there?"

"Do you remember when we were kids?"

Nate smiled. Of course he remembered. He was still a kid. Perpetually sixteen or so. "Yeah, I remember that."

"Remember that time I stole that Corvair from the neighbors?"

"The white one?"

"Uh . . . no. The black one," I said.

"Right, right," he said. "That was a classic."

"Remember how we drove it around the neighborhood, but never crossed the same streets? So that we made a big, growing box around the house?"

"No."

"Well, that's what I did. That's what I want you to do, but do it the opposite way. Go wide and then narrow down to the house. Anyone following you is going to become obscenely obvious."

"And what do I do if someone is following me?"

"You know where the county jail is?" I said. Nate gave me a grave look. "Don't go in. Just park in front of it and then call me."

"That's *just* like stealing a Corvair," he said. He got into the Lincoln and I watched him pull out into traffic. He'd be fine, I knew that. It didn't hurt to give him some advice now and then. Particularly since I was going to spend the rest of the evening risking my life, it seemed like a fair trade-off.

When I got back to the Charger, Fiona was filing the serial number off of the .380 she'd taken from Clete.

"Thanks for the backup," I said.

"I watched the whole thing," she said. "That woman in the Cadillac was a true menace."

"Zadie looked awful," I said.

"She just had radiation," Fiona said. "She's not supposed to look good."

"What's worse, the cancer or the cure?"

"You should tell your mother to stop smoking," Fiona said.

"I have."

"Then you've done your job," she said. There was a hint of sarcasm in her voice.

"This isn't about me," I said.

"Michael," she said, "you can always try harder for the people you love. Look at Bruce. He went to prison for his mother. And he had his finger removed, too. And he robbed a biker gang. All for his mother. That's devotion."

It was something. I wasn't sure it was devotion.

"He told Nate that he's robbed hundreds of banks," I said.

"Maybe he has."

"Doesn't that make him worse than me?"

Fiona put the .380 into her purse but didn't say another word.

She didn't have to, I suppose. Any woman filing the serial number off of a .380 has her own set of rules.

"We need to go to a hardware store," I said. "You up for an arts-and-crafts project?"

"I love it when you sweet-talk me," she said.

12

When you ambush somebody, it's not merely about surprise and suppression. You can only surprise someone once in a given situation. You can only suppress someone for as long as they feel you hold the upper hand in terms of power. With deficient manpower and against a worthy opponent—which is typically the scenario that would necessitate an ambush—that isn't a very long period of time.

A proper ambush surprises, suppresses and then creates institutional control.

Provided the goal of the ambush isn't to kill every single person, the result of a successful operation is to strike fear into the enemy, to make them think you know their every move and already have a counter in place. This creates fear and suspicion in the rank and file, which leads to paranoia in the leadership.

In an organization like the Ghouls, where by definition the membership is made up of felons, a successful ambush will act like a magic pill. Suddenly everyone is looking over their shoulder. And the big boss man in the gold Lincoln? He's looking for a scapegoat just to quiet the troops.

I already knew that was his specialty.

The man in the gold Lincoln burned down the stash house and killed the men who ran it. He also killed Nick Balsalmo (or likely ordered the job), probably just for having the Ghouls' drugs and for not being forthcoming with the information on Bruce Grossman.

Or, well, allegedly he'd done those things. Anyway, I couldn't help but assume that life was not looking particularly rosy for Clete, Skinny and the Hobbit now, either. At the moment it wasn't my largest concern, as Sam, Fiona and I were busy prepping the Grossman house for the eventual arrival of the Ghouls. We were in the process of moving most of the Grossmans' furniture out into the backyard when Sam asked me an important question.

"Tell me something, Mikey," Sam said. "What creates that old-lady smell?"

"Palmitoleic acid," I said.

"What's that?"

"A fatty acid found in your skin," I said. "Old people make more of it. Their skin sloughs off and suddenly everything smells like a wet book."

"In this context, what's old?"

"Over forty-five."

We set the sofa down outside, next to where Fiona was working on her arts and crafts. She had several small sheets of plywood that she'd cut into the shape of cat's heads. Beneath the head of the cat, the plywood descended into a spike. The plywood was painted black and glass beads, inlaid into tinfoil, were placed along the face to form reflective eyes. She'd made ten of these cat heads. The plan was to plant them throughout the house—in the living room, the entry hall, and since the kitchen was inexplicably carpeted, the kitchen, too. In the dark, they would reflect any ambient light and give the impression that the house was filled with wild, or, preferably, feral, animals.

If you want to scare someone, anyone, make them think they are surrounded by animals. The mammalian brain does not like this. The mammalian brain will ask you to flee. The mammalian brain doesn't care if you're a biker or a priest or Britney Spears.

I picked one up and caught the fading sun with the eyes. "Nice work," I said.

"I know," Fiona said.

Sam sniffed his arm. "I'm good, right?"

"I think alcohol and suntan lotion probably help neutralize the odor," I said. "Or I'm just used to the way you smell. So I guess you really can't be sure, Sam."

"I'm sure," he said.

"Then you're fine."

"Fiona?" Sam said.

"You smell like mothballs and sweat-soaked back hair," she said.

Sam's cell rang before he could respond to Fi, which

was good news. Anything to reboot him was always good news. He stepped inside to take the call, so I took a moment to survey our work. We'd moved all of Zadie's living room furniture into the backyard. Fiona was putting the finishing touches on our slight bit of diversion. Oh . . . and there were two huge custom choppers with engines that sounded like F-16s parked just a few yards from the open sliding glass doors that led back into the house.

Our plan was simple enough: We turned off the power to the inside of the house at the fuse box, but left the outside lights on, brought the garage door down and parked Zadie's station wagon in the driveway. I even went outside and put some magazines and junk mail into the mailbox. The Ghouls were likely to hit at night, particularly in this neighborhood, so we'd wait for them. When they broke in, they'd find a house filled with animals . . . and then they'd get the real animals.

Sam came back outside a few moments later holding a tube of Jergens hand lotion. He squirted out a large dollop of it and began working it into his hands, forearms, elbows and up under his shirt.

"It's too late," Fiona said.

"It's never too late," Sam said. He put his arm under Fiona's nose. "How's that smell? Huh? Like pure, blue air, that's how."

"Where'd you find that?" I asked.

"Guest bathroom," Sam said, "along with five hundred rolls of toilet paper and a tube of Bengay."

"I'd check the expiration date," Fiona said. "I found sour cream in the refrigerator that went bad in 2002."

Sam smelled his hands. "Fresh and clean doesn't have an expiration date, my friend. Good is still good. Still real good."

Fiona picked up one of the cat heads and poked Sam in the gut with the pointed end. "Why don't you apply some of that lotion to those fatty acids?"

I could watch Sam and Fiona fight all day, except that eventually Fiona would stop playing around and Sam would get hurt, so I put a stop to it by asking Sam who was on the phone.

"That was my guy Philly in the FBI," Sam said. "I decided to step over the DMV and just go straight for the crime database, you know? Besides, Bruce dropped off their roll. I thought maybe they'd have worked through it by now and could just deliver all the information we could ever need."

"Your guy at the DMV is that bad?"

"You have no idea," Sam said. "Anyway, Philly says the Lincoln is registered to Cindy Connors."

"None of the three guys in the Lincoln looked like a Cindy."

"Yeah, that didn't sound right to me, either," Sam said. "So I had Philly run Cindy's name. Turns out she's the sister of one Lyle Connors. Also one Jeb Connors, one Kirk Connors and one Victor Connors, all of whom have resided in federal custody at least once."

"Lovely family," Fiona said. "It's like you and Nate, Michael."

"Funny," I said.

"Anyway, Lyle seems to be the big guy," Sam said.

"How do you figure?" I asked.

"He's the only one not in prison currently."

"Your deductive powers are amazing," I said.

"That's Uncle Sam's intelligence training right there," he said.

"Can you get a sheet on him?"

"My guy is gonna e-mail it to me as soon as he can sidestep all of his superiors and the electronic filters," Sam said. "So, probably first thing tomorrow."

"And people wonder how terrorists slip into the country," Fiona said. She gathered up all of her cat heads and went inside.

"Any word on Maria?" I asked.

"Nothing," Sam said. "I had my guy run her, her mother, her stepfather, gave him everything I had from the DMV, but you might be surprised to learn that the number of Maria Corteses in the world prevents a thorough accounting. But look, José said she'd call. I believe him."

"Why?"

"He's lived in the same house for fifty years. If you can't trust someone who has lived in the same place for fifty years," Sam said, "who can you trust?"

That sounded reasonable and I said so. If she didn't call, there was still a good chance she'd show up at Nick Balsalmo's funeral and we could talk to her then, whenever that might be. The Ghouls were smart enough not to say anything directly about Balsalmo's death even when they thought they were safe at their clubhouse, but I still felt like Maria knew something. Enough, anyway, that between her and the information we were compiling, plus what we intended to do that night, we might be able to keep the Ghouls away from Bruce Grossman.

I had to hope, at least.

The key to a successful operation is patience. If you're going to work in intelligence, you must be willing to survive boredom. You must become the king of the mundane.

As a kid, if I got bored I'd go into the garage and find something to blow up. I was particularly fond of using Aqua Net as an accelerant, particularly while using Nate's bicycle to reenact Evel Knievel's failed jump over the Snake River Canyon. The best way to defeat boredom, I learned, was to create conflict. Even if I got in trouble, at least it was better than having nothing to do at all.

That course of action wasn't available to the three of us while we waited for the Ghouls to arrive at the Grossman house. Sam and Fiona took turns providing a lookout, which involved crouching in the juniper bushes along the side of the house for twenty minutes at a time, which, after nine hours, caused the two of them to start bickering.

For a while, their bickering was actually entertaining. And then the fifth hour slipped by. And then the sixth. And the eighth. At 2:30 A.M., Sam started actively complaining.

"You know what would be good right now?" he asked.

"A muzzle," I said.

"Steak 'n Shake," he said. "I'm starving."

"If you're still hungry in the morning," I said, remembering one of my mother's favorite sayings, "you can have breakfast."

"What time is morning, technically?"

"After we deal with the Ghouls," I said.

"And why are you so sure they'll get here before I die from hunger?"

"These guys aren't dumb," I said. "They'll pull Bruce's name off of the Web site and if they have to hit every Grossman in Miami, they will."

This quieted Sam for a moment.

That moment came to an end.

"What I don't get," he said, "is how these guys can wear these outfits every day."

We were both dressed in jeans, black T-shirts and denim vests that had our colors on the back. We were part of a gang called the Redeemers. Sam told me they were big in Oregon. That they used to be part of a Bikers for Christ pack but they splintered off and decided to be Bikers for Meth instead, but kept their name because it sounded badass. They'd tried to colonize in Florida and the FBI had quashed them and then took over their identity for undercover use. They were now Bikers for J. Edgar Hoover.

"I'm comfortable," I said. And I was. We were both sitting on chaise lounges beside the choppers in the backyard, so that when the Ghouls came, we'd be able to kick-start them and barrel into the living room on cue.

"How many vests do they have? Don't they begin to stink? I mean, hypothetically, how old are these guys? Forties, right? They're gonna get that smell, Mikey, that's all I'm saying. I just don't see these guys doing a lot of laundry."

Just as I was about to tell Sam that everyone eventually had to do their laundry, that that was the one thing that made us all equal, I heard the growl of a muscle car on the street. Drive a Charger long enough, you begin to know how every decent American muscle car sounds from about fifty yards away. My guess was Camaro. 1976.

Fiona texted a confirmation: *Bad men in a bad car*. She scurried into the yard seconds later.

"They're here," she said. "They just rode once around the block."

"How many?" I asked.

"Two," she said. "In an old Camaro. Quite lovely, actually."

"How are you sure it's them?" Sam asked.

"It was fairly easy," she said. "They were the only people on the street in a yellow and black Camaro with racing stripes on the hood casing out the old woman's house."

"For now," Sam said. "They figure out this is the right place, they'll call in reinforcements."

"Then we'll just have to be effective in our job," I said. "Let's mount up."

Fiona selected her weapons. She was determined to use Skinny's shotgun, if only for ironic purposes, so she had that as her primary and one of those nice guns she sold the Cubans on her leg.

"Fi," I said, "let's try not to light up the entire neighborhood."

"You have no faith in me," she said.

"Untrue. I have absolute faith in you. Which is why we don't need to send hollow-points into the Chabad house down the street."

"I know my role, Michael," she said and then slipped back out into the juniper bushes.

When you're planning an ambush, it's also important to know where everyone is going to be shooting from, should the situation demand such action, so that the ambush doesn't turn into a friendly-fire incident. As soon as the Ghouls busted into the house, Fiona would come in behind them while we roared in from the backyard.

Inside the house, we had set up a few obstacles—

large pieces of furniture—and surprises—the feral
cats—to ensure that we would find ourselves in an L
formation and that the Ghouls would be disoriented.
We'd funnel the Ghouls into the long leg of the L, directly in front of Sam and me, and up against a make-
shift wall we'd built with furniture, so that instead of
being able to slip into the kitchen, they would instead
be pinned. Fiona would be on the short leg of the L, at
a right angle to us. We'd be shooting the Ghouls head-
on, Fiona would be shooting them in the side of the
head or the back.

It was a brutal thing to consider, but then ambush-
ing someone isn't about rose petals and whale songs.
We had two core advantages working in our favor: We
were trained and our goal was not to kill anyone, much
to Fiona's disappointment.

Sam and I rolled up to the open sliding door, our
front wheels just an inch from the thick shag carpeting
that must have been fashionable at some point in the
past, but not a past I readily recalled.

It took a few more minutes, but we finally heard the
Ghouls approaching. The Camaro they drove had an
engine that sounded like someone choking to death on
a bag of glass. Fiona texted: *They've parked behind the
wagon. Examining the car. Just cut the tires.*

"Look alive," I said to Sam and then texted Fiona:
Guns?

Fiona texted three words back: *Bats, hammers,
knives.*

All that meant was that they hadn't yet pulled out their guns. You don't go to kill someone without a gun, usually. Beating someone to death, or stabbing them, leaves a lot of evidence around. But then, of course, if they actually needed the stuff Bruce had taken, perhaps their goal was not to kill him now, only to torture him until he gave them back their money and property.

Coming up the walk now.

We'd locked the front door, but I knew that wasn't a deterrent, especially since the front door was equipped with a lovely, decorative, frosted tempered-glass inlay, which to criminals is like leaving a plate of cookies and a note that says, "Come on in!" on the front porch. Unlike regular glass, tempered glass won't break into huge, artery-cutting shards when it's smashed. Instead, it shatters into oval-shaped pebbles. It's also five time harder than regular glass, which is great if you're worried about grandchildren running into and slicing their heads off but doesn't really take into account bikers with bats, hammers and knives.

Fiona texted: *They're duct-taping the glass.*

Duct tape usually makes you smart. And while no one could reasonably compare anyone in a biker gang to one of the generation's guiding intellectual lights, they knew crime.

Or at least they knew how to break glass quietly.

Taping off the section of glass you're interested in breaking will dull the sound of the breaking glass. Instead of a shatter break, the glass will receive a concussion break, so that the glass will spider out from the center point, but only the center point will be broken straight through. When executed correctly, the broken glass will stick to the duct tape and all your cosmopolitan criminal will need to do is remove the tape and there, as if by the magic of criminal ingenuity, will appear a hole.

Unless, of course, you're an idiot and you duct-tape the glass and instead of hitting it just enough to break the small section, you hit it so hard that you put your entire bat through the window and crush the whole plate, thus completely counteracting the intelligence of using duct tape in the first place.

There was a loud crash of breaking glass, followed by another text from Fiona: *Idiots.*

A dog began barking a few doors down. But since most of the people in the neighborhood had been asleep since about eight fifteen—if you eat dinner at four thirty, you tend to go to bed pretty early—and most of them probably took their hearing aids out at night, no one even bothered to yell at the dog to be quiet, never mind popping outside to find out why two bikers were breaking into the Grossman house.

Fiona texted one last time: *They're going in.*

I counted to fifteen and then heard the sound I was hoping for: "Ah!" A minor shriek of fear and surprise. Followed by: "Uh!" The sound of fear and surprise is an evolutionary caution for humans—it's the easiest sound for us to discern, even in a crowded room.

Frighten a human and other humans will know immediately. When you're about to ambush someone, it's the first thing you hope to hear, as it puts you at an immediate—and involuntary—advantage. You're not afraid. They are.

"Did you see that?" one of the men managed to get out. He was trying to whisper, but whispering when you're afraid is nearly impossible. Unless you are speaking directly into someone's ear and can thus modulate your voice down below the normal decibel level we can easily perceive, whispering tends not to work.

A normal whisper, in a controlled environment, where your emotions aren't heightened, is thirty decibels.

A whisper of fear?

You might as well use a bullhorn.

"What the hell is that? A dog?"

"I don't know. Maybe a big rat."

"Man, no one said anything about animals."

I heard the sounds of cracking glass as the men traversed the entry hall looking for the switch, heading directly in the path of the living room.

As soon as their shadows fell into the living room, Sam and I kicked into gear, thundering the choppers into the house, filling the small home with light and violent noise. The two men screamed—or at least they appeared to scream, since we couldn't hear them over the engine noise—and dropped their bats as they attempted to jump away and cover up.

It's only natural.

If you suddenly see a motorcycle charging toward you, particularly inside an enclosed space, after already being frightened by wild animals, you're going to forget just how tough you are.

Sam and I pinned the two Ghouls up against the wall of the kitchen, our front wheels coming to a stop right above their knees. If we'd wanted to, we could've gunned our engines at any point and broken their legs.

But that was probably the least of the men's worries, since Sam and I both had our guns pointed directly at their heads, too. Fi came walking up with her shotgun.

"Hello, boys," she said. She was about ten feet from the two men. From that distance, if she shot one of them in the head, it was likely the bullet would sail straight through and hit the other guy, too.

They didn't say anything.

"How is Clete doing?" she asked.

13

When you're in the business of information, it's important to be able to identify messengers. In the spy world, this means that you can spot the one person in the crowd who is waiting for you to walk up and say, "The eagle has landed."

In the human body, those messengers are hormones. Just like spies, they are dispersed into the community—in this case, the bloodstream—to be funneled toward the appropriate targets in order to provide necessary information. The first hormone ever identified was adrenaline. This happened in 1901. By 1904, adrenaline was being synthesized in the laboratory for medical use, as in counteracting anaphylactic shock.

When it occurs naturally in the body, adrenaline dilates blood vessels and air passages, which increases muscle performance and mental acuity for short periods of time.

As in, for instance, the brief period of time it took Fiona to beat the living crap out of Clete.

When you don't use your adrenaline in an appropriate amount of time—as in what was happening to the two Ghouls pinned to the wall inside the Grossman home—you might find yourself feeling nauseous, shaky and disoriented.

You might even find yourself unable to answer simple questions, which was also the case with the two Ghouls.

The men had calmed down slightly, now that they understood they were not being attacked by wolves or lions or angry domesticated house cats, and perhaps also now that they saw what they were up against. It wasn't the first time either of them had had a gun pointed in their direction, that much I knew. Both of them were at least thirty-five, though they each had a particular look. One was tall, maybe six-three, and his forearms rippled with veins and muscles. I couldn't really imagine him hitting the gym all that often, so my guess was a healthy steroid diet and a couple of months in County were his standard regimen.

The other was shorter by a few inches but probably weighed sixty pounds more, all of it in his stomach. He had a long black goatee that hung down to the middle of his neck and his cheeks were pocked with acne scars. Surprisingly, he looked tattoo free, which probably meant that under his clothes he was painted head to toe.

"I hope Clete isn't having any problems walking," Fiona said. "Did you notice him limping?"

Still nothing.

"Answer her," I said.

"I don't know who you are," the tall one said to me, "but you're already dead."

"That must have sounded scary the last time you said it," I said. I turned to Sam. "You scared?"

"Petrified. I just hope I don't lose control of my muscles and let go of the brake."

Both Ghouls tried to take a step back, but just ended up hitting their heads against the wall. I took a quick inventory of their bodies and determined that both the big one and the fat one had guns—the big one in his waistband, the fat one shoved uncomfortably into his right front pocket.

If you want to accidentally shoot off your genitalia, the best place to put a gun is right where these two had theirs. If you want to hide your gun from plain sight, since I imagined neither of these gentlemen had permits, trying to stuff a nine into your belt makes it difficult to do things in public. Like, say, standing for any length of time.

"You still haven't answered her," I said to the men.

"You broke his back," the fat one said. "Is that what you wanted to hear?"

"Yes," Fiona said.

"What kind of club lets a woman bust up one of their own?" I said.

"Two," Fiona said.

"Two," I said. "I stand corrected. Who knew the Ghouls were getting so soft?"

There wasn't much either of them could say to that. It was true. Even they knew it.

They just didn't know Fiona.

"All right, boys," I said, "my partner—" I looked at Sam and noticed that he had a kind of John Wayne thing going with his face, a sort of half-scowl/half-smirk thing, so I said, "Duke is gonna take both of your guns. You make any moves, my lady peels your caps back. No questions, just brains on the carpet. We clear?"

Both Ghouls nodded.

Sam dismounted his bike slowly, like maybe he thought he was John Wayne, too. And instead of a horse, he had a bike.

"Hands up," Sam said and I thought I detected a bit of a twang.

The Ghouls raised their hands and Sam removed their guns, then patted them down and came out with two knives, a sap, a bag of meth, a needle, and two wallets bulging with cash. He handed me the wallets and tossed the rest of his haul out the screen door.

I opened up the wallets and looked at their driver's licenses. The tall one was named Clifford Gluck, the fat one Norman Gluck. Brothers, though presumably by different fathers since no Punnett square could produce these two reliably. The pictures on their licenses were both a good ten years old and neither Gluck looked particularly threatening. Clifford, who at thirty-seven was the older of the two, had short hair and was wearing a tie in the photo. He also wore a smile so wide you'd think maybe he just won the free dinner from Chili's at the company picnic.

Norman, who was thirty-five, was still pudgy and bearded, but he also wore a tie, though I had the sneaking suspicion his dress shirt was short-sleeved. The term "middle manager" was made for Norman.

Weird. Both of them, in the recent past, looked like guys who worked all week in a mindless corporate job and then really cut loose on the weekends by playing paintball and watching horror movies. How you went from that life to being in a biker gang was a mystery to me.

"Which one of you is Clifford?" I asked.

"That's funny," Clifford said.

"Hard to tell from these pictures," I said. I handed the wallets back to Sam so he could have a look.

"Nice ties," he said.

"Look," Clifford said, "we weren't here looking for you. Whatever your problem is, it's not with us. You let us go, we forget the whole thing."

"You a lawyer?" Sam asked.

"I look like a lawyer?" Clifford said.

Sam flapped the wallet in Clifford's face. "You do here," he said.

"What's your story?" I said to Norman. "You only talk when he says so?"

"I ain't got nothing to say," Norman said. "Either shoot us or fuck off."

"So he's the lawyer," Sam said to me.

Clifford had a tattoo on his hand of a little girl's face. It was a professional job, nicely shadowed, plenty of detail. It didn't exactly make him look tough. And not even bikers think highly of pedophiles, so my suspicion was that it was probably his kid. That told me that somewhere inside Clifford, combined with the fact that he once wore a tie for his driver's license photo, there lurked a human being who could be reasoned with.

I decided to make our first move.

I reached into one of the saddlebags on my bike and pulled out a handful of patches belonging to the Ghouls. Both Clifford and Norman visibly stiffened with anger. It was silly, really. They were just patches. But then, I guess if I was being tortured by bad guys in some foreign land and they showed me an American flag that they were desecrating, maybe I'd feel anger, too.

"These belong to you," I said, and stuffed them into a pocket in Clifford's vest. "I got another three, four hundred more of them. I also got your constitution and every other piece of paper you morons created. You want 'em back?"

Clifford looked at Norman. Norman looked at Clifford. It was actually kind of cute. Big bro and little bro trying to figure out the right answer.

"Yeah," Clifford said.

"Five hundred large," I said.

"Check or money order?" Clifford spat back at me. "Or can I give a credit card?"

"Maybe you haven't figured it out," I said, "but I've already done your dirty work. Bruce Grossman is dead. And now I've got all of this Ghoul crap. You want it, you gotta pay my cost or you let the Redeemers take over this territory. Simple as that."

"Bullshit," Norman said.

"He does speak," Sam said.

"Shut up," Clifford said. "Let me think."

"Let's see a body," Norman said. "Otherwise it's bullshit."

"Shut up, Norm," Clifford said. "This isn't your call."

"It's not yours, either," Norman said.

From a sociological standpoint, it was fascinating watching Clifford and Norman. Here were two brothers, maybe with different mothers, maybe with different fathers, maybe they were born in test tubes in a lab in Geneva, but whatever, they were brothers somehow and they clearly were having a power struggle. Having it in public with guns in their respective faces made it all the more interesting. At least when Nate and I had such issues in front of other people, we were usually the ones holding the guns.

Clearly, however, neither Gluck was a shot caller. One might have more rank than the other, but it would be up to Lyle Connors no matter what happened here tonight. Perhaps he gave one of them more latitude than the other—say, perhaps one was allowed to execute Bruce, the other was in charge of the acid bath—

but my sense with these two was that this was more of a kidnapping than a murder. They wanted their money, drugs and paraphernalia back . . . and then they'd kill Bruce.

Clifford and Norman continued to argue over who could speak while the three of us just watched. It was moving to the level of performance art until Fiona made it stop.

"Mommy must hate it when you two fight," Fiona said. "Why don't I shoot you both and the one that can still talk can be the official spokesman?"

That quieted them down.

"Listen to me, boys," I said. "We're all in the same boat here. The Banshees hired Grossman to hit us both. I got that much out of him. He was actually pretty forthcoming after Duke took off his ear."

Sam tried to act nonchalant and menacing at the same time by squinting one eye and surveying Clifford and Norman's ears.

"The fat one," Sam said, "he'll take a saw. That's a pretty thick membrane he's got there between his ear and his head. Might need to get something electric involved."

"See what I mean?" I said. "Grossman didn't have a thick membrane, so he gave up pretty quick. He got lucky one time robbing you, because you're stupid enough not to have gone digital. What the hell were you people thinking, keeping a bunch of paper around?"

"Institutional stupidity," Sam said. "That's my guess."

That would have to stand as the answer, as neither Clifford nor Norman was piping up. It didn't matter, really, since they had no say. They were just messengers. Just adrenaline. But they would take the message back, that much I knew.

"Grossman, he didn't fare so well trying to hit our stash. I cleaned up my mess and now I'm happy to make a deal to get your mess taken care of, too, before you gotta deal with the Banshees."

"What about you and the Banshees?" Clifford said.

"They don't have territory we want," I said. "They're moving H and girls. That doesn't interest us. Their disrespect does, but I'll work through that. They'll get theirs."

"Oh, indeed, pilgrim," Sam said. "The Redeemers will be redeemed." He was using that John Wayne voice again. It wasn't really working. Maybe it was the use of "pilgrim" as a pejorative. I gave Sam's chopper a light kick just to let him know that maybe he should remain quiet if he was going to be using that particular vocal disguise.

The fact was, getting the Banshees and the Ghouls into a conflict served everyone's purposes—everyone that was on the right side of the law, at least. People getting hustled by the Ghouls were usually in no position to go to the police, so business was conducted as usual. But when two gangs go to war, that's something the police and the FBI have a real interest in. There's a lot of illegal secondary activity involved with a gang war.

"Boss will want to see a body," Norman said. "Until then, fuck off."

"Norman, shut the hell up!" Clifford said.

"The offer is five hundred K," I said. "That's cash."

"At least that much was taken from us," Clifford said.

His numbers were a little off—or Bruce's were—but I decided not to note the difference publicly.

"I got some of that, too," I said. "But that money's dirty. Probably the FBI has every other serial number written down. I want five hundred K fresh. I don't care where you get it. Twenty-four hours from now, I want a response. Or I keep all the money, piss on your colors, and drop your paperwork off with the first Johnny Law I see."

Clifford shook his head. "No disrespect," he said, and I actually felt like he meant it, "but you won't see a dime and I'll probably be killed for not killing you. Then you'll have Ghouls on your ass until the end of time. Every Redeemer in the country will have a target. No one wins here."

"The Banshees do," I said, because I hated to admit it, but it seemed like Clifford had a valid argument. "This is probably what they want. We kill each other over their job. They practically led us right to Bruce Grossman in the first place. How long did it take you?

A day? Two? I'm gonna guess that house fire out in the Glades wasn't an accident."

"We walk out of here, we never saw you," Clifford said.

"That what you told Nick Balsalmo?" I figured I'd play that card, particularly since it wasn't like Nick Balsalmo was some undercover operative. He was a drug dealer, which meant that by definition, he knew people. "That guy wasn't terrible. But I saw what you guys did to him. That didn't look like a nice transaction."

"I got a kid," Clifford said. He showed me his hand. I wondered if he was also showing me his hand metaphorically, if this was how he got out of every sticky situation. Who's going to kill someone with a tattoo of their baby daughter on their hand?

"Just let me shoot them," Fiona said.

Well, there was one person . . .

"You'll be looking for my girlfriend, anyway," I said. "We're already at war. You just didn't know who you were fighting."

Clifford considered my response. It also made sense.

"A body," Norman said quietly. This time Clifford didn't disagree.

"Proof of death," Clifford said. "You give us Grossman's body, maybe the boss will listen, work something out, save us all a lot of problems. You bring us his head, we can do business."

"His head is gone," I said. "He's not in a lot of big identifiable pieces."

Both men nodded with an odd sort of personal re-flection. This was shop talk. We could have been talk-ing about the best oil to use in our choppers for all the emotion any of us displayed.

"We heard he was missing a finger," Norman said. "That's how we'd know who he was, make sure we didn't grab the wrong son of a bitch. You think you could get that hand?"

I looked at Sam. This was going to be something he'd need to be in on, for sure. "Duke, you leave one of his hands intact?"

"Yeah," Sam said, but he didn't sound filled with confidence. "Yeah. One of them."

"All right," I said. "You two go back to your boss and tell him we'll drop the hand off at Purgatory tomorrow. Any shit goes down, I blow the building up."

"Anything else?" Clifford said.

"Yeah," I said. "Tell your boss that if he doesn't like my terms, or crosses me up, or tries anything shady, I got a guy who is pretty handy with a pair of bolt cut-ters sitting outside Cindy Connors' house right now and wherever she goes, he goes. Forever."

"You got a name?" Norman said. Suddenly he was Chatty Cathy.

"No," I said. "I'm just a Redeemer."

I rolled my chopper back about a foot and so did Sam. The Brothers Gluck now had enough room to move, but nothing to make moves with.

"She gonna shoot us if we take a step?" Clifford said.

"No," I said. "But watch your kneecaps. And when you get outside? Try to be quiet. I don't want one of my guys to get jumpy and accidentally cap you both."

I watched Clifford and Norman walk back down the hall. When they got near to Fiona, she smiled at both of them. "Tell Clete he should have let me use the bathroom," she said. "And that it's not polite to call women names."

Neither said anything, which was wise.

Once outside, they climbed into their Camaro and drove off slowly. No shouts. No curses. No shots.

"That was fun," Fiona said. Her face was flushed and a little sweaty. I'd seen that look on her face before, but not from this angle.

"Yeah," I said.

Fiona brushed past me, essentially rubbing most of her torso against my right arm in the process, and made her way to the wet bar in the living room. "I'm dying of thirst," she said.

Once she was out of direct earshot, I turned to Sam. "You know where we can get a human hand?"

Sam exhaled through his mouth. His eyes bulged a bit, but apart from that he didn't seem unduly bothered by the question. "I got a buddy I can call," he said.

"Good," I said.

"Might be hard to find one with a missing finger."

"We can work around that," I said.

"We?" Sam said.

"Fiona can," I said.

I heard rustling behind me and turned to see Fiona in the middle of the living room with a bottle of rum in her hand. "Cocktails, anyone?" she asked.

14

As a rule, Sam Axe didn't really care for the sight of dead bodies. Spend enough time in the military, particularly if you happen to be one of those people who gets called to do the jobs no one else wants to do, and the chances are you're going to see a few bodies. There's no good way to depersonalize the experience. A human being is a pretty unique animal and even if you don't see a part of yourself in every person that passes you on the street, subconsciously you make that connection. It's what keeps most people from killing: simple human empathy.

And of course Sam had killed people in the course of doing his job. He hadn't enjoyed it. He didn't actively seek out the experience. But he had orders and he had to trust in the chain of command. If he was to kill someone it was because someone deserved to die. That's what makes a good soldier.

Still, being around dead bodies creeped Sam out. Yet there he was at eight thirty in the morning, just a few hours after dispensing with the Ghouls, in the parking lot in front of the Miami–Dade County Medical Examiner's Office. It was a bizarre place to be at any time of the day, but even more so in the morning, since from his car Sam could see the traffic along Northwest 10th Avenue streaming by, no one even really bothering to look frightened. Didn't they know they were driving by a slew of dead bodies? True, they were driving through an area that was densely populated with medical buildings—Jackson Memorial, Highland Park and Cedars were all over there—but still. Just a few yards away, people were toying with dead bodies!

The other weird thing was that the ME's office was located on a side street off of Northwest 10th called Bob Hope Road. Somewhere, Bing Crosby was laughing his ass off.

Sam was to meet his buddy Brenna Fender in fifteen minutes. She worked in the ME's office as a nurse, but that was just a ruse: She'd been in the office for the last six months doing an undercover operation involving black-market organ sales.

Normally, Sam would steer clear of someone like Brenna, but they'd gone out for drinks on a couple of occasions and Sam honestly liked her—she knew the value of Sam Time and wasn't all clingy about things. Truth be known, Sam was of the opinion that maybe Brenna wasn't clingy about anything—she just liked to have a good time and then go on back to sniffing out the dark underworld of spleen sales.

Anyway, she was the one person Sam knew who

could give him a hand, literally. And maybe, if things went well, they'd hook up later in the week. See about catching a movie or getting a beer or six. Provided he lived through the week. Or maybe that would be the payoff from tangling with a bunch of murderous bikers: an evening on the town (or on the sofa) with Brenna Fender.

Sam's cell rang, breaking his reverie.

"Is this the person who came looking for me?" a woman's voice said after Sam answered.

What an incredibly stupid question, Sam thought. This was not a person who knew much about staying alive. "That depends," Sam said. "Is this the person I'm looking for?"

There was silence while the woman—who Sam presumed was Maria; hell, he prayed it was Maria, since the idea of more than one person making a phone call like this gave Sam vertigo—pondered her answer.

"I guess," she said after another couple of beats. "You know Nick? Is that what this is about? Because I haven't seen him in, like, a week. I don't even know where he is."

The problem with most people is that they feel like the best way to get through an interrogation is to give way too much information, as if being forthright will somehow absolve them of any guilt, even if what they are saying is an absolute lie. Hadn't she spoken to her stepfather? Didn't she know what Sam already knew? Was she this stupid?

"No," Sam said, "but I know a friend of his. Bruce Grossman. That name mean anything to you?"

There was a silence again as Maria tried to work through the equation. Bruce Grossman probably wasn't the most important name for her to remember, especially if Nick kept his business and personal life separate, but they had dined together. That meant something, didn't it? Didn't breaking bread count for anything anymore?

"Yeah," she said. "They did time together, right?"

"Right." He decided to stay consistent and said, "Bruce's dead now, is the thing. Bikers got him. Did him ugly. Any idea why?"

Another long pause, which didn't engender a lot of faith in the answer when it came. "No," she said.

Something Sam learned in the military is that if you're not happy with an answer, give it back to the person in the form of a question. The weak-minded were incapable of dealing with this technique and invariably ended up giving you the very information they were attempting to conceal.

So Sam said, "No?"

"Not really," Maria said.

"Not really?"

"Who are you again?" Maria said.

"Chuck Finley."

"And how did you get my name?"

"Nick was one of the last people Bruce called before he got done in," Sam said, figuring the girl had seen enough of those cold case and forensics programs to put the rest of it together. She was scared, clearly, and had some story she'd practiced, since nothing was coming from her in any sort of natural way.

"Nick said they were doing some business together," Maria said.

"They were doing some business together?"

"Bruce sold him some drugs."

"Bruce sold him some drugs?"

"Okay, fine," she said. "Bruce just gave them to him. Okay? Is that what you were looking for?"

Maria made Sam worry about the future of America. If everyone was as easy to pull information from as Maria was, what chance did the country have of beating back terrorism? Didn't anyone lie convincingly anymore? Didn't anyone just hang up the damn phone? It's not that he was upset with Maria, only that he recognized in her a failure: People just didn't know how to shut the hell up. Which maybe would create jobs in the future, actually, Sam came to reason. People like himself wouldn't become obsolete because people like Maria would need to be protected.

"Where's Nick? I need to talk to him," Sam said, deciding to just keep moving forward, irrespective of what he thought Maria should know already, since if she was going to play stupid, he was going to play stupid, too. Just to even the playing field.

"He's dead, too, okay? For like a few days. You talked to my stepdad, you know this, right?"

"Oh," Sam said, "right. I just wanted to hear you say it."

"You sound like my stepdad," she said, which made Sam kind of proud.

He liked José, especially since it turned out he was true to his word, even if Maria's call was a few hours overdue. He wasn't sure Maria was the same type of person, so he said, "What made you tell the Ghouls Nick had their stuff?"

There was another of those grating pauses, but this time Sam thought he heard sniffling. "Nick, you know," Maria said quietly, "he wasn't a good person."

"He wasn't a good person?" Sam was annoying himself with the repeated phrases, but it was a system that seemed to work with Maria, so he just kept tossing the lines out there, figuring when she stopped biting, he'd change the bait.

"He liked to hit me," she said. "Broke my collarbone. Messed up my shoulder. One time, I told him I was pregnant, just to get him to leave, right? Instead, he tried to kick me in the back. So when I heard there were people looking for a big haul of drugs, you know, stuff that wasn't normal in our neighborhood, and that they were offering a reward, I might have said something."

"You set him up to be killed?"

"No!" she said, her voice rising. "No. No. I just thought, you know, these guys would mess him up. Get their drugs, mess him up, I'd get some money and, you know, get a new life. Get out of Little Havana."

Sam saw Brenna Fender come out of the front of the ME's office. She had a plain brown bag in one hand and her purse in the other. She wore a cute pair of scrubs—Sam thought all scrubs were cute, really, a lasting impression from being in a secret military hospital in Bucharest and meeting a very friendly nurse while pumped full of Dilaudid—and didn't seem to bother with looking inconspicuous. Brenna stopped next to the garbage can and chatted with the three other people in scrubs who stood there smoking. Sam never understood how you could work at a hospital and still smoke.

"How much did they give you?" Sam asked.

"They were supposed to give me twenty grand," Maria said, "but they only gave me five hundred up front and then came by my parents' place and told me to get out of town before they did me like they did Nicky."

"They said that?" Sam said. When Maria didn't respond, he added, just for the sake of continued clarity, "They told you they'd do you like they did Nicky?"

"Yeah," she said.

"Where are you?" Sam said.

"Out of town," she said.

"Out of town?"

"I'm in the Ranchero, okay?"

"Don't go anywhere," Sam said. "I'll send someone to come and get you."

"And what?"

A good question. He'd have to find out if Madeline

was prepared to take on more houseguests. He imagined Maria might be somewhat surprised to find Bruce Grossman living and breathing when she got there, but he'd deal with that later. Maria Cortes was now evidence.

"You get to use a bathroom inside and we'll keep you safe," Sam said.

"Who are you again?"

"Not the cops," Sam said. "Ask your stepdad."

Silence. And then: "Okay," she said, "but my dog comes, too, okay?"

Oh, Madeline would love that. "Thirty minutes," Sam said and then had to hang up. A woman with a human hand in a brown bag was knocking on the passenger window. He unlocked the door and Brenna Fender slid in. She smelled of formaldehyde with a hint of Chanel No. 5. Classy.

"How are you, Sammy?" she said. All smiles. Big eyes. Friendly. Like this was something she did every day. She set the bag down between them.

"I'm good," Sam said. He wondered how much a hand weighed. Two pounds? Three?

"Which is why you need this hand?" No smiles. Small eyes. Not terribly friendly. Like this was something she did every day and then, later, showed up in uniform to arrest the perpetrators.

"Complicated situation I'm working on," Sam said. "You've heard of the Kobayashi Maru, I assume."

"No," she said. That was good . . . since Sam was pretty

sure the Kobayashi Maru was something from *Star Trek: The Wrath of Khan*, which he'd watched in bed after getting home from dueling with the Gluck brothers.

"Well, then, I'm afraid I can't divulge the exact reasons behind our need for the hand. For our eyes only and all that, you understand."

Brenna regarded him with real skepticism, but Sam decided he'd stay firm. She'd already brought him the hand, after all, so she couldn't be feeling too moral about the situation.

"Take a look, then," she said. "Make sure you got what you need."

Sam was afraid she'd say that, but he opened the bag and took a peek. "Yep," he said, "that's a hand."

"Anything else you need, Sam, before I lose both of my jobs?"

There was one thing that vexed Sam. "Who did this belong to?"

"You read about that pimp who got cut up by about ten of his girls a few nights ago?"

"Must have missed that one," Sam said.

"That's because it wasn't in the paper," she said.

"No?"

"Nope." Brenna got out of the car but didn't close the door for a moment. She looked both ways, presumably to make sure no one was watching, good guys or bad guys, and then poked her head back inside. "They never found the body," she said. "You have a good day now, Sam Axe."

15

There's no easy way to fake your own death anymore. Used to be all you needed to do was squirrel away the cash you'd need to make a new life, get a fake passport from your local forger, and then roll your car off a cliff in the middle of the night. Twenty-four hours later, and a continent or two away, you'd be sitting on a white sand beach, or at an outdoor café, or just beneath the majesty of the Alps, plotting your next life.

Now, just getting through security at the airport would be a challenge. Sneaking into Mexico might not be terribly difficult, provided you're able to get to a border city without leaving a trace of your real self along the way—there are cameras everywhere now, even if you're not aware of them—which is where the complications might arise. And then once you're in Mexico, provided you don't die of swine flu, or get kidnapped, or get murdered in the crossfire of a drug war, you'll realize that Mexico isn't exactly paradise lost and you'll want to find greener, less smoggy, less dangerous pastures. And then you're back to the same problem of traditional air travel.

Terrorism may have made air travel annoying for those of good legal standing, but it's made it damn near impossible for those attempting to fake their death. Minus that, there's just so much DNA we all leave behind now—fingerprints, hair fibers, saliva, urine—that if you really feel like you need to fake your death, you might want to consider actually killing yourself.

At least that way you won't get caught.

In Bruce Grossman's case, he was actually taking his death pretty well. He sat wedged between his mother and my mother on the sofa and watched one of those "I have terrible taste and need help" programs on HGTV. Maria Cortes and her dog were asleep in Nate's old bedroom. After Maria got over her initial surprise at seeing Bruce alive and well—Sam had to convince her that he wasn't a ghost and that no one was avenging anyone, at least not in my mother's house—she quickly made herself comfortable. Apparently sleeping in a car had left her exhausted.

Fiona, Sam, Nate and I were in the kitchen, along with a brown bag containing what would be the proof of Bruce Grossman's death, provided someone was able to chop the appropriate finger off. More important, however, if this was all going to work, I needed to make sure Maria was going to be the witness Bruce would need to really disappear safely. As it stood now, I felt like we could forestall the Ghouls by giving them

the hand and then selling them their own goods back.
Maybe they'd engage in an even bloodier war with the
Banshees, but eventually, because he was Bruce Grossman and couldn't keep his mouth shut for more than
ten seconds at a time, he'd tell someone about how his
best score was the time he robbed the Ghouls twice.
And once with a spy! And then, well, then one day the
Ghouls would show up at his house with bats, and
acid, and there wouldn't be a way out.

Bruce Grossman had to give the Ghouls back the
works and then he had to disappear. And somehow,
we needed to keep Zadie safe, too. The best option was
not one I suspected Bruce would leap at.

"Do you think Maria would go on the record about
Nick?" I asked Sam. "Because if she can deliver the evidence that there was a bounty on him, along with what
Fi recorded at Purgatory, there's probably enough to
get Bruce and Zadie into protective custody."

"Yeah," Sam said, "but he did rob that stash house.
You think the FBI is going to smile on that?"

"They wanted him once before, didn't they?" Fiona
said.

It was true. Back when he was in prison they'd offered to make him a consultant, but he was a different guy then. Younger. Dumber. And probably more
skilled. Plus, his mother wasn't dying. If he went into
their hands now, she'd get the best medical care.

"I don't know," I said. "He doesn't seem like much
of an asset anymore." In the living room, Bruce was

arguing with my mother over whether or not tile floors or hardwood were the better flooring for the couple on the television, particularly since neither had the hall-marks of something he kept calling "divine design."

"It's not about whether or not he can rob banks still," Sam said. "They'd probe him. Find out what made him rob banks. Find out his psychology."

"I wonder what they'd make of me?" Fiona said.

"You might create a whole new field of study," I said.

"Mikey, how many guys have the forethought to let someone whack off their finger in prison for insurance money?" Sam said. "He might seem like an old man in an ugly sweater, but that guy, he's a treasure trove for some headshrinker."

"And you, Michael," Fiona said. "What would they do with you?"

"I think they're already doing it," I said.

All of what Sam said was certainly true, but when mixed with the issues at hand, there was some massag-ing that was going to need to be done. If Bruce refused custody, or if the FBI didn't care to relocate him, and if the Ghouls came up with the $500,000, which would be enough to take care of Zadie no matter where Bruce might have to run to, it wasn't as if Bruce would have zero problems toting $500,000 in loose bills. If they actually paid up, we'd need Barry to facilitate a few banking issues, none of which were legal, which might then put Bruce in a perilous situation yet again.

There was also a pretty good chance the Ghouls might not find the story about the Banshees setting this into motion all that believable. Oh, certainly the Gluck brothers believed it, but they weren't running the show. Someone like Lyle Connors, a guy with a gold Lincoln, he might see the flaws in it. If we really wanted to pit these two groups against each other, we'd have to rob the Banshees, too, and make it look like the Ghouls did it.

Depending upon how this afternoon turned out, all options were open, which is what I told Fiona and Sam. I didn't really say it to Nate, because he wasn't listening. He was busy staring inside the bag at the hand.

"Let me know when we get to do that robbing of the Banshees bit," Fiona said. "I have a few new moves I'd like to try out. And a few things I'd like to buy, too, so perhaps you'll let me blow their secret vault."

"I'm not so sure these guys have a secret vault," I said.

"Everyone's got a secret vault," Sam said. "Right? I know I do. Working on getting that undersea lair together, just in case the North Koreans send a bunch of nukes our way."

I didn't answer Sam for fear that he might honestly be building an undersea lair. Instead, I focused on Nate, who was oblivious to everything going on around him, save for whatever he saw in the brown bag.

"Nate," I said, "you're either a part of this or you're not."

"You know, it doesn't really smell," Nate said. "At least not from here."

Great.

I checked the clock on my mother's 150-year-old microwave. It was ten thirty. Nate was due to take Zadie to radiation in about forty-five minutes. We had to get moving in all areas.

Which included the task at hand, so to speak.

"All right," I said, "who wants to cut off the finger?"

No one jumped at the chance.

"One of us has to do it," I said.

Still nothing.

"It's not as if it's even a hand anymore. It's completely disassociated from the body. And it belonged to a bad guy, right, Sam?"

"Right," he said, "but candidly, Mike, it's hard for me to disassociate the hand from the person if you keep reminding me it used to be on a person."

"Would it be easier if he said it was on a goat?" Fiona said.

"Was that you volunteering?" Sam said. "Ladies and gentlemen, Fiona Glenanne will be performing her magical finger-removal trick now. Fiona?"

Fiona, for the first time in her life, didn't have a quick missile to launch in Sam's direction.

"What about you, Nate?" I said.

"I'm not the globe-trotting assassin," Nate said.

"I'm not an assassin, Nate," I said. "I'm a spy."

"Right," he said. "Sorry. My mistake. I'm not the

globe-trotting spy who occasionally killed people for the government. Is that better?"

"It's just a hand," I said, a truth I was in the process of reminding myself when my mother walked into the kitchen.

"What are all of you fighting about? I can hear you all the way in the living room."

"Which is ten feet away," I said.

"What's in that bag?" she said. She reached for it but I pulled it toward me.

"Nothing, Ma," I said. "Go back to your television show. They're just about to reveal the new countertop."

"Michael, I have thirty strangers and a dog in my home right now, all as a favor to you. The least you can do is tell me what else you've brought into my house. What could be worse than what is already here?"

Since I'd been back in Miami, my mother had been shot at, ambushed and pulled in several directions by forces foreign and domestic. She's aware that I work somewhere between the law and disorder. She owns a shotgun. She married my father, which was like sanctioning an emotional Cuban Missile Crisis for the whole of the 1970s and most of the 1980s.

So she can handle herself.

"It's a dismembered hand," I said.

"And why is it in a brown bag on my counter?"

"We need to chop off one of the fingers, so that it matches up to Bruce's hand," I said. "And then we're going to use it to fake his death."

"And what's the problem?"

I looked from Fiona, to Sam, to Nate—three people who knew their way around a crime scene, generally—and landed back on my mother. "No one really wants to chop the finger off."

"Oh, for goodness' sake," she said. "Didn't any of you ever work on a farm? Fiona? Didn't any of your relatives have a farm in Scotland?"

"Ireland," she said. "And no. Most of my family worked with their hands to steal things from other people."

Ma regarded Sam. "Madeline," he said, "you have to understand my rich regard for the sanctity of human life. And that I had chicken fingers for dinner last night."

She didn't bother reproaching me or Nate. She just shook her head and said, "Nate, reach into the drawer beside the sink and hand me that electric carving knife your father used to like to use on Christmas."

When Nate didn't budge—and when I didn't let even a breath escape me—she sighed, went into the drawer under the sink, a place where the past evidently stood still, and came out with the GE Electric Carving Knife I remembered from every major holiday between my birth and leaving Miami directly after high school. My father and mother used it to cut any meat thicker than a slice of Italian salami and, occasionally, my dad used it for minor home repairs—it worked great for cutting into drywall—and anytime something in the Charger needed to be severed, which accounted for the odd saw marks I found on various hoses, tubes and fabrics when I refurbished the car not long ago.

Because it was made in the 1970s, the knife needed to be plugged in. Fortunately, it was still attached to the mud brown ten-foot extension cord Dad had put on it sometime before the first *Star Wars* movie. The dual blades looked dull, but that might have just been a mirage from the caked-on grease, animal blood and remnants of duct tape, since when Ma plugged it in, the 120-volt motor roared to life and the blades looked positively deadly.

The noise got Bruce off of the sofa. He examined the knife, examined his own gnarled stump and said, "That should do the trick."

"Bruce," I said, "why don't you have a seat before you get hurt?"

"What's the worse that could happen? I lose a finger?"

He waited for the laugh to come and when it didn't, he seemed honestly disappointed. I had a feeling it wasn't the first time he'd used that line.

"Uh, Ma," I said, "let's think about this."

"Oh, Michael," she said, which was her code for: Shut up. She took a look at Bruce's hand, noted the approximate spot where his pinkie stopped—he had only a nub above the knuckle—and then sliced right through the finger of a dead pimp.

She calmly turned off the electric knife, unplugged

it from the wall and set it in the sink while all of us stood by.

"Michael, you'll wash the knife?" she said.

"Sure," I said eventually.

"And maybe spray some Lysol on the countertop?"

"Will do," I said. "Anything else?"

She thought for a moment. "Nate, when you go out to take Zadie to her appointment, will you stop by the grocery store and pick up a gallon of milk and one of those nice rotisserie chickens?"

Nate waited for me to say something, as if I could provide any kind of insight into this person who apparently had abducted our mother. I was just hoping she didn't get wise and turn the electric knife on me. "Sure," I said. "Nate can do that. Can't you, Nate?"

"Sure, Ma," Nate said. "Whatever you need."

Ma and Bruce went back into the living room. Their show was over, so they switched to Food TV and settled in for thirty minutes of heart-pounding excitement via a show about a guy who only eats absurd quantities of weird food.

"So," Sam said.

"We're not going to speak of this," I said.

"What just happened?" Nate said.

"Fi?" I said.

She looked at the hand there on the counter for a few seconds and then said, "Doesn't it look too fresh?"

"We'll put it in some dirt," I said. "So it looks like we just dug it back up."

"Best-case scenario," Sam said, "you just tell them we cut even more off while torturing Bruce for information. The Ghouls will appreciate that."

"Okay," I said. "Fi, you're going to stay here and watch over Bruce and Maria and make sure my mother doesn't cut anything else, okay?"

"Lovely," she said. "Say hello to my friends at Purgatory."

"I'm not going to do that," I said. "But stay near the phone. We end up in a situation that needs your special attention to detail and explosives, I'll call you."

"Goody," she said. "Am I excused now, professor? Because I must learn how to eat a giant pizza and it appears there's a show all about that on the television at this very moment."

"Dismissed," I said.

I watched her walk back into the living room. She plopped herself into a chair and immediately fell into the program on the television. For a woman who weighed ninety-five pounds on a day when she wasn't armed, she sure did like those cooking programs.

She'd have her hands full with Bruce and Maria, but I didn't think for a moment that she'd be unable to take care of it. Especially since there was no sense in dragging a dead man out in public, lest he do something stupid, so keeping Bruce at the house was of the utmost importance. And since I knew he'd happily stay wherever Fiona was, I was confident that at least that avenue would be clear.

This was particularly important, since if the Ghouls knew *where* Bruce's mother's house was, they might have known *who* his mother was as well. With Nate taking Zadie to the doctor by himself, there was less of a chance that something beyond my control might happen. The Ghouls would be unlikely to make a move on an old woman since even bikers had a modicum of ethics.

Sam and I were going to handle the Ghouls and that meant Nate would handle Zadie.

"Nate," I said, "you need to get Zadie into and out of that radiation appointment unscathed. Don't let her talk to anyone. Don't let her mention her son. We have no idea who might be on the Ghouls' payroll by now, so you take her in, you watch her, and you take her right back out. You feel like anyone is on your tail, head for the police station. Just like last time. Okay?"

"How about if I notice anyone," Nate said, "I'll just bring them here and Ma can handle them. I mean, Michael, we need to talk about what just happened. Right? We avoid it, isn't it like all that crap we avoided as kids that now has you all screwed up? Isn't that right?"

"No, that's not right," I said. "We just pretend it didn't happen."

"If I end up with post-traumatic stress," Nate said, "it's on you."

"Fine," I said. "I'll make sure I have a trauma nurse waiting for you here when you get back."

"You don't find what just happened odd, Sam?" Nate said.

"Nate, my boy, I have seen things that would make you question your own sanity. Papua New Guinea, fall of 1988, I saw a band of pygmies fell an elephant with spears and then climb into the elephant through its mouth and then out its backside," Sam said.

"What?" Nate said. "What?"

"That's my point," Sam said. "I didn't sleep for three days after that. So your mother? Just a quirk. She'll probably think she dreamt it herself. People under stress, Nate, they do crazy things. I ever tell you about the time I saw a toddler lift a car off of his father? Side of the road. Kid knee-high to a grasshopper just picked a car right up. Damnedest thing. Right, Mike?"

"Uh, right," I said. "Nate, look, just do this job for me. Keep her safe. You can do that. I know you can."

Nate huffed and puffed a bit, but it was clear to me he was just happy to be part of the group. Even if it's hard to depend on him to always do the right thing, it's easy to depend on him emotionally. He is, after all, my brother and if there's one thing I know about Nate, it's that he wants to perform well. It's not his fault that he doesn't always have the natural ability.

Well, he might have the natural ability, actually. It's not his fault he's cultivated it toward stupidity on occasion. Not everyone is cut out to be a spy.

Besides, people tended to like him. Like Zadie, who put her arm through Nate's and let him guide her outside to his car, which left me and Sam alone in the kitchen.

"*Superman*," I said.

"No, no," Sam said. "I'm just a regular guy like you, Mike."

"No, that story. About the kid. That's from the first *Superman* movie."

"You saw that?"

"Everyone saw it," I said.

"Not Nate, apparently," Sam said. "Anyway, what do you think? We get out of this alive?"

"I don't know. I didn't read my tea leaves this morning." I pointed down at the hand. "Maybe we get a palm reader over here and find out what his palm says and go from there."

"Good idea," Sam said. "Maybe get a Ouija board, too?"

I laughed. It felt pretty good. "This won't be the hardest thing we've ever done," I said. "All we need to do is walk into a hornet's nest and not get stung."

"It'll be like that time in the Sudan," Sam said. "Remember that?"

"Which time?"

"1993?"

"Were we there then?"

"Oh," Sam said, "I can't remember anymore. But what I remember is that we ended up as the last two people alive and we fought our way out using nothing but our good looks and sharp wit. And then we had mojitos afterward. Ring any bells?"

"That was in Venezuela," I said. "2002."

Sam closed his eyes. "Oh, yes," he said. "I do remember. Lotta water under our bridge, Mikey."

I pulled out a drawer and found a big Ziploc freezer bag and slid the hand into it. "Well," I said, "then let's go make some waves."

16

Just as it's nearly impossible these days to fake your death, there's also no easy way to prepare for your likely *actual* death other than recognizing that it's one of several possible outcomes. Normal people don't usually possess this ability. It's an existential conundrum and most people can't even define "existential" or "conundrum" much less handle the philosophical questions of being. When you're trained by the government to kill, you get a crash course in desensitization. From the first day of boot camp onward, you speak of death—both the death of your enemy and your own.

From the cadence chants of basic training to the man-shaped silhouettes you're taught to fire at, to the new virtual-reality simulations that allow you to take on an entire city of people, you become inured to the common fear of death that a sane person might have. You're willing to walk into enemy fire because you've already survived.

The result of this training is a series of skills that

most humans really shouldn't want, including the inability to feel fear when they really should.

Give this training to the wrong person and you just might give a platform for a burgeoning sociopath.

Give this training to the right person . . . and you end up with me and Sam riding howling hogs down a street in Miami, our saddlebags filled with paperwork and patches belonging to the Ghouls Motorcycle Club and one human hand, minus a severed pinkie.

We pulled up across the street from Purgatory and parked our bikes. It was barely 11:00 A.M. and traffic was light, but regular. Even a cop drove by once, but he didn't bother to slow down. A block up the street was a 7-Eleven. A block down the street was a McDonald's. There was a used-car lot within fifty feet of where we stood. And at 11:00 A.M. all had customers.

In front of Purgatory was the gold Lincoln and two bikes. Clete wasn't holding up the front door, for obvious reasons, but his replacement looked to be cut from the same piece of cloth. Neck tats, arms the size of barrels, sunglasses, jeans, a bat.

He also had an iPhone, which he was playing with and therefore didn't notice me and Sam staring directly at him. Not even the Ghouls can get a decent security detail, apparently.

"That guy is pretty scary-looking," Sam said. "If a softball game breaks out, we're done for."

"Be careful," I said. "He might also text you to death."

"Kids," Sam said, "they love the texting."

Another cop drove by. It wasn't that odd, really. It wasn't the best neighborhood in the city, or the worst, but it was also only about a mile from a substation where, a few months earlier, a delusional gangster had decided he'd go Terminator and try to shoot several police officers using a paintball gun. It didn't go well, which told me that at least the cops were pretty good shots.

"Nice that there's a legal presence here," Sam said. "It would be a real shame if they just let a criminal organization roost here under their nose."

"Alleged criminal organization," I said.

If the Ghouls were really savvy, they'd call the cops as soon as we got anywhere near them. We were in possession of stolen property, after all, and they knew we'd be strapped.

Which gave me an idea.

I called 911.

"Yes, hello," I said, "an eighteen-wheeler holding about ten cars on it? Toyotas? Maybe Hondas? Anyhoo, I think they are foreign cars? Well, I just saw one of those crash into one of those big apartment buildings on 142nd Avenue. Pardon me? Oh, the south part. Maybe south and to the west. There's a huge fireball. Such pretty colors!"

Before I could continue with the show, the 911 operator told me authorities were on the way and disconnected me.

"Nice," Sam said. Twenty seconds later, we heard the first sirens in the distance. An ambulance raced by us shortly thereafter, followed by two fire engines and two police cars.

"Good response time," I said.

"Unless one of us needs an ambulance," Sam said.

I tossed my cell phone into the street and watched as a second ambulance drove right over it, crushing it to pieces. Making a prank call to 911 isn't advisable. They tend to track you down, arrest you, and put you in jail. It would be slightly more difficult to find out who I was with my burner crushed into the pavement. It was okay, though; I had another phone on me and another fifty or so at home.

After the authorities passed on by, traffic returned to normal. A city bus rolled by. A low-flying plane pulled an advertisement. A man pushing a taco cart walked in front of Purgatory but didn't even look up from his feet.

Not a great time to open fire on a city street. Which was good. I didn't want to get shot.

But sometimes, you need to let the neighbors know you're home.

"Do you want to shout the hard-core thing or should I?" I asked Sam.

"I've got a couple of lines I've been working on," he said.

"Please, no more John Wayne," I said.

"You'll have to wait and see." We both pulled out our guns. He shouted, "Wagons forward, ho!"

I fired two shots into the gold Lincoln, taking out two of its tires. Sam fired two more shots, taking out the other tires. The guy guarding his iPhone surprised us both by throwing down his iPhone and ducking for cover, which was the smart move.

"*Hondo?*" I said.

"It was on television."

I stepped out into the middle of the street, my gun on the crouching Ghoul. I could see that he was trying to get something out of his pants; his gun, most likely, which proved yet again how stupid it is to keep your gun in your belt, since it's not very easy to retrieve it when you're crouched down hoping to save your life. I walked a few more steps and then said, "Don't do that."

The Ghoul looked up at me. "Don't do what?"

"Your gun. Don't take it out and don't try to shoot me with it. If I wanted to kill you, you'd already be dead. And if you're not careful, you're liable to blow your right testicle off. So stand up and pull your gun out slowly and then toss it into the gutter."

Sam had followed me but was still about ten yards behind me. Cars swerved around him on the street, but no one seemed to be the least bit surprised that two guys with guns were stalking around. The man with the taco cart was about a block away, but hadn't bothered to turn and look at the commotion. McDonald's was still serving up Quarter Pounders. Gas was still being pumped. For some reason, the rest of the Ghouls hadn't stormed out of Purgatory yet, which led me to believe they were expecting a show, which probably meant that the Ghoul on the street was not their most treasured asset.

"Man," the un-treasured asset said, "you're in the wrong place," but he tossed his gun into the gutter anyway.

"People keep telling me that," I said. "And yet, here I am. I wonder why that is?"

"Do you know who you're shooting at?" he asked. He sounded incredulous. It was the default sound of tough guys who can't believe other people don't think they are tough.

"If you have to ask that question," I said, "then the answer is yes. Now, run inside and tell your boss that there are some bad men outside who'd like to talk to him."

The Ghoul didn't move.

"He gonna shoot me in the back?" he asked. He indicated Sam with a lift of his chin.

"I don't know," I said. "Duke, you gonna shoot him in the back?"

"Out here, due process is a bullet," Sam said, which only confused the Ghoul.

"That means no," I said, though that wasn't true. It just meant Sam had also seen *The Green Berets* recently. "But walk backwards if it makes you feel more comfortable."

The Ghoul did just that, but before he made it up the steps to the door, it opened and Lyle Connors stood in the doorway. He wore a linen summer suit with no tie. His hair was parted conservatively to one side and his face was freshly shaved.

He walked down the steps, shoved the doorman aside and stepped past both Sam and me to look at his car. He walked around it twice, checking for damage. There wasn't any, apart from the tires. He seemed content with that.

"Feds don't knock anymore?" Lyle said to me.

Not what I was expecting.

"Wouldn't know," I said. "But I figured trying to get past your man at the door would be difficult."

Lyle laughed. "You send a woman to do your work yesterday and you're scared of one guy? The FBI isn't what it used to be."

"I don't know who you think is FBI," I said, "but it ain't us."

"No?" Lyle said. "Since when are the Redeemers back in business in Florida?"

"Since Oregon stopped being profitable," I said. "And since we got tired of having the FBI wearing our colors and riding our bikes."

Lyle regarded me for a few seconds. I couldn't tell if he was looking for cracks in the veneer or if he was just trying to apply some silent pressure, see if I or Sam started babbling or backtracking.

"That so?" he said. "How come we haven't seen any soldiers? You two and your crazy woman, that's the whole unit?"

"You don't believe me, that's your business. Doesn't change the fact I got this." I reached inside my vest and pulled out the Ziploc bag now holding Bruce Grossman's hand—or, well, the hand portraying Bruce Grossman's hand—and dropped it at Lyle's feet. I'd shoved a couple of the Ghouls' patches into the bag, too, just for effect. "I also got a bunch of maps in my saddlebag that list all the safe houses you got between Tallahassee and here. That's gotta be worth something to someone, right, Duke?"

"You got that right," Sam said. "Put it on eBay. Get the Banshees and the feds to bid against each other."

Lyle's right eye twitched. He didn't look horribly mad, but that twitch wasn't because he was over-caffeinated.

"What's your name?" he asked me.

"You can call me Jasper."

"Okay," he said. "Tell me something, Jasper, what makes you think I'll do business with you?"

"It doesn't matter. Either you do business with me or you don't, I'll still get what I want. Professional courtesy, I came to you first, seeing as the Banshees tried to screw both of us. You don't pay up, we take over this territory. I make my money either way."

"I'd like to see you try," Lyle said.

"You would," I said. "Because we'd be wearing your colors. We'd go door-to-door looking for old ladies to smack up. We'd set up shop outside elementary schools to move meth. We'd pimp out thirteen-year-old girls.

And when the police got close? We'd take them to your safe houses. We'd leave a trail out to your processing plant in the Glades. We'll go out to Sturgis, Oklahoma City, Houston and we will shoot at people. And when we get tired of that? We'll come back here to Miami and maybe we'll kill some Cuban Mafia don and then a cop and a rabbi and a priest and maybe we'll kidnap Dwyane Wade. All in your colors."

That twitch? A full-blown blink.

Lyle scratched absently at his neck until a thick red line rose up from the skin just above his Adam's apple. "Maybe you're not feds," he said. Lyle looked down the street, his eyes squinted into narrow slits, like he was trying to make out something very important in the distance that he knew should be there but wasn't. "You hungry?" he asked. "I can't negotiate on an empty stomach."

I looked at Sam. He gave a quick shrug. "We could eat," I said.

Lyle reached down and picked up the bag with Bruce Grossman's hand in it. He unzipped it, pulled out the Ghouls' patch, and then took a moment to examine the evidence before dropping it back onto the pavement with a dull *thwack*. "Buster," he said to the doorman, "get rid of this. Put it in the incinerator. Chop it up. Feed it to your pit bull. Just get rid of it."

"Got it," Buster said.

"And tell the boys inside that I'm going down the street to McDonald's for a business meeting," Lyle said, "and that if I don't come back in an hour, they should go kill everyone named Grossman in Miami. Got that?"

The McDonald's down the street from Purgatory didn't have a Playland. It was one of those recently renovated McDonald's that looks like a Starbucks slathered in trans fats and encourages people to come in with their laptops and spend the day eating French fries and Oreo McFlurrys while sucking down the new McDonald's espresso drinks.

So even though there was no area dedicated to screaming children, there were plenty of postcollegiate men with messenger bags and wire-rim glasses working on their novels or résumés or letters to *Parade* magazine about the state of Jennifer Aniston's romantic relationships.

Lyle insisted on buying us lunch, so Sam and I found a circular table with a good view of the door and of Lyle. Sam watched the door. I watched Lyle. Not that we didn't trust him, aside from him being a murderous biker gang leader, but it just made good sense to watch the hard target and pay mind to any soft ones coming through the door.

It probably made sense to Lyle, too. We'd already proved that we weren't afraid of taking him on in what would otherwise be the sacred ground of Purgatory, and that we could predict his moves enough so that we were waiting on his men at Zadie's. Going to McDonald's? That wasn't something I could have honestly assumed.

He walked back to the table and set down a tray loaded with food and for a couple of minutes the three of us ate in silence, Lyle protecting his meal prison-style, with one arm wrapped around the entire tray. He was a Big-Mac-large-fries-and-an-orange-drink kind of guy.

No apple pie.

No McFlurry.

No salad.

He was Old School.

Time for recess.

"Since when do Ghouls wear suits?" I said.

"It's about diversification," Lyle said. "New business models. I can't walk into a business meeting dressed like you two. You'll find that out soon enough, Jasper. You wear a suit, you're untouchable."

"And yet you leave all of your most important stuff in a stash house somewhere?" I said. "You ever hear of a computer? You ever see Bruce Grossman? Man was almost seventy. You got jobbed by a guy collecting Social Security."

"He got you, too," Lyle said.

"Correction," I said. "He tried to get us. You know what he stole from me? Shoe boxes. You know what was in those shoe boxes? Shoes. He stole my shoes. Little bit of money. Little bit of drugs. Not like how he took you down. He bullied you. Treated you like his stepson. Us? He got what we left out. Plain and simple. And he paid for it. Boy, did he pay for it. Oh, it took us some time to find him, but we didn't have to go torture and kill someone else to get to him. Didn't have to put no bounty out in Little Havana. We handled our business. While you were busy making house calls in Little Havana, Bruce Grossman was already in the dirt. We had to sit and wait on your asses. So you got taken by an old-ass man and by us and by the Banshees. You're 0-for-3, hoss."

Lyle took a long drink from his orange soda. Here was a man not used to being talked back to, getting talked back to.

The twitch was coming back.

"You can change an environment overnight, but you can't change the people inside of the environment immediately," he said, his voice careful, measured. "Lessons have been learned." He talked like someone who'd been reading manuals on corporate leadership.

"Expensive lessons," I said.

"You think you'll be able to do whatever you want to do for the rest of your life?" he asked. "Me? I'm fifty years old. My brothers are all doing time. You think I want to spend the next thirty years doing fed time? So I'm changing the way the Ghouls handle their business. Keep us protected and keep us in business. I'm clean. I intend to stay that way. Maybe I've got some dirty friends. Even Obama has a few of those, right?"

It was nice talk, but they'd killed Nick Balsalmo.

They'd killed the men working the stash house. And they would have killed Bruce. But now I understood why, even though we'd threatened Clifford and Norman, we weren't met by a dozen men with guns when we approached the bar.

"So, what," Sam said, "you want some kind of corporate alliance with us? That what we're talking here?"

Lyle laughed. "No. No, I do not. What I want is for you to stop embarrassing my people. Your arrival in town is a good object lesson. The ranks are bloated with idiots and cowards. Ten years ago? You'd already be dead. But you move fast. You're nimble. I like that. You probably have my whole operation rigged, right? Know where all my weak points are. That's how the Ghouls should operate, but no one here has any idea how to run a business. None of these guys ever worked in the military, so they've got no sense of structured command. All of them were raised on *The Godfather* but didn't have sense enough to get mobbed up. So here they are with the Ghouls, happy to rally, happy to run meth. Living and dying over their colors. Me? I'm thinking internationally. I'm thinking about the brand. You understand?"

If I had to make an informed guess, it would be that Lyle Connors had not only read a few books on management structure but was also taking classes in the University of Miami's continuing education program.

Maybe it was a condition of his parole.

Maybe he really wanted to change the way the Ghouls did business.

Maybe he just had nothing to do on Wednesday nights.

"You talking about action figures and lunch boxes?" I asked. "A Ghoul under every Christmas tree?"

"I'm talking about a binary approach to business," he said and then I was sure he was taking night classes. "We do the drug game and then we have a legit side that isn't just to keep the RICO off our asses. Not just kids' charities once a year or bumper stickers like the Angels do. I'm talking about fantasy camps, video games, reality television shows. Taking this game to the next level."

"You realize you'll need to stop killing people," I said. "No one wants to go to fantasy murder camp."

"You'd be surprised," Lyle said.

"I'm never surprised," I said.

"Point is, men," Lyle said, "there's a role in this for you if you want it."

"For us?" Sam said. "I thought you said you weren't looking for alliances."

"I'm not. I'm looking for someone to teach my people how to ride right. You two—and that woman—you got your roll down. I don't know how many people you got backing you every time you go out, but the three of you come out like an army, like *the* army. You want this territory? You buy in. No war. No bloodshed. We make a deal, we make the Redeemers legit again, no one thinking you're FBI. Everybody wins. Or you give up that Redeemer shit and those colors you've been holding, they become yours."

Lyle Connors was smart. I had to give him credit for that. He recognized a situation that was undermining his ability to govern and he acted. Did he mean anything he said? It was hard to tell. There was nothing stopping him from letting us buy in and then killing us five seconds later. There was nothing stopping us from buying in and killing him five seconds later. But by making this offer, he forced our hand. What he wanted to know was if we were opportunists or if we were just in it for the quick score.

"No, thanks," I said.

"No, thanks?" Lyle said. He sounded pretty sincere. I hated to let him down.

"We don't go into business with Ghouls. Never have. Never will. I'd sooner mount up with bin Laden. And anyone coward enough to invite us in is no one I want to be associated with." I stood up, which got Sam to stand up, too, though somewhat reluctantly. He was still working on his Quarter Pounder. "You got until midnight tonight," I said. "Five hundred thousand, cash, or it's a war you can't win."

"Show up at midnight," he said, "you'll have your answer."

Real cool.

No pressure.

A man who has spilled blood on the street before acting like: *What's another couple bodies?*

Before we walked out, Sam grabbed up his burger and a handful of fries. "Thanks for lunch," he said. "Good luck with that video game. Let me know when you book the Ghoul-themed cruise, too, okay?"

17

When you're out for revenge, you tend to lose the ability to think beyond the act of retribution, the fleeting emotion of righting a real or perceived wrong. While I didn't care for the existence of the Ghouls Motorcycle Club, the fact was they hadn't actually tried to come at me. They'd only come at Bruce Grossman because he made the error of robbing the wrong damn stash house. That he wanted to give back what he couldn't use, while admirable, didn't make him any less guilty of a crime, nor did the fact that he robbed them in order to provide medical care to his dying mother.

When you live in a civil society, you must adhere to the rules. Without rules, only the toughest, most aggressive of the pack will survive.

Bruce Grossman wasn't tough.

Bruce Grossman wasn't particularly aggressive.

Bruce Grossman wasn't even a great bank robber. He was just a lucky one, whose adventures had become romanticized lore, such that even Fiona had heard of him and the FBI wanted to employ him.

And now I had to protect him, which meant two things.

I needed to dispose of the Ghouls and everything of theirs that Bruce possessed. If I could sell it all to the Ghouls, that would make for a perfect order of life, but I knew well enough that come midnight, there would be war.

Bruce Grossman had to stay dead. If he managed to get arrested again, the Ghouls would know, and then he would be dead again, but with a headstone and appropriate services.

I sat in my mother's living room and explained both of these things to Bruce. He nodded his head once but then didn't say anything at first. Sam and Fi were in the kitchen working on a laptop to get some pertinent information and pretending not to listen to our conversation, though every few seconds I heard Fiona sigh or mutter something like, "Oh, just put him on the rack, for God's sake!" Luckily, Bruce's hearing wasn't so swift.

Zadie, my mother and Maria kept themselves busy at the kitchen table trading *People* magazines back and forth. I could tell my mother was getting jittery from the lack of tar in her body but she was somehow managing to not smoke inside her own home. My bout of childhood bronchitis cursed her.

"So," Bruce said, as though he'd downloaded my thoughts, "you grew up in this house?"

"I did," I said. "Nate, too."

"And your dad, where's he?"

"Dead," I said. "But he haunts the linoleum in the laundry room."

"And you liked it here?"

"Can't say that I did."

"Your brother? Did he?"

"No," I said. "It wasn't always the happy place it is now. We only put the razor wire in for you."

"But this is home, right?"

"For better or worse, Bruce, this is home."

"I go and work for the FBI," Bruce said, "I never see home again. I lose everything that's me. What if they stick me in Phoenix or something? Me and Sammy the Bull get to hang out together? Is that what my life would be? I'd rather be in prison."

"Sammy the Bull is in prison," I said.

"See what I mean?" Bruce said.

"Listen to me," I said, "you go to prison, you'll be dead in twenty-four hours. There are Ghouls in every prison in the country. You turn to the feds, they'll put you up somewhere where your mother can get help and maybe you have to sit around talking about robbing banks all day, or maybe you don't do anything, because what you have here of the Ghouls, all of this information, that's one deep cover the feds don't have to run. You'd be saving lives. Most notably your own and, for a while, your mother's."

That seemed to resonate with Bruce. "Okay," he said, "okay. I get that."

"One thing," I said. "If Sam can swing this, you have to recognize that your life of crime is over."

"What about, say, I see a pack of gum at the CVS and no one is around?"

"You wait at the counter with your fifty cents."

"What about running red lights? I still get to run red lights every now and then? What about cheating at cards? Is that against the law?"

Bruce was getting agitated, just as I figured he would, which is why I left out one key ingredient to this conversation. One dangling carrot that I knew Bruce could not resist if offered.

"There's maybe one thing you could do," I said.

"Yeah? Cheat at bingo?"

"How would you like one more score?" I said.

"I've seen this movie," he said, but, oh, there was a spark in his voice, so I played it out.

"Never mind, then," I said. "Sam will call the feds, see what we can work out."

"Let's not be hasty," Bruce said. "You haven't even told me the score."

I smiled. "That's the super criminal we know and love," I said. I waved Sam and Fi over.

"Finally," Fiona said, this time loud enough that everyone could hear.

Sam sat down between Bruce and me on the sofa and handed him the laptop. "You recognize this?" he asked.

On the screen was a two-story house in what ap-

peared to be a nice neighborhood. The lawn was cut.
The windows had white shutters. In the driveway was
a Volvo SUV. You could almost hear the sound of a gold
dog barking and small, adorable children telling their
J.Crew-model mother that they were bored.

Suburbia personified.

"Am I supposed to?" Bruce asked.

"It's a stash house belonging to the Banshees," Sam
said.

"Nice taste," I said. I looked at the address. It was
a neighborhood only a few miles from my mother's
that was once just open fields but was now a housing
development absurdly called Coconut Commons. Still,
the homes were the kinds thirtysomethings imagined
in their Pottery Barn dreams.

"The Banshees just know how to protect their inter-
ests," Sam said.

Sam was probably correct. Houses in nice neighborhoods don't get robbed as often as houses in bad neighborhoods and just because the Banshees were criminals,
it appeared they at least read the newspaper more often
than the Ghouls did. Pick up the *Miami Herald* on any
given day and you're more likely to see a home invasion
robbery in the toughest parts of Liberty City or Miami
Gardens than in the toniest areas of Key Biscayne.

"So you never cased this place?" Sam said.

"No," Bruce said, "it doesn't look familiar."

"What's inside?" I said.

"My buddy who did undercover? He says they have

a couple houses like this all through Miami that they grow marijuana in."

"In?" I said.

"Yeah," Sam said, "they gut all the rooms and turn the entire place into a hydroponic farm. Maybe have two or three guys living in the place, tending to the crop."

"What's there to steal?" Bruce said.

"Finally," Fiona said, "someone asks a good question."

"Well, that's the thing," Sam said. "They don't keep cash here, or if they do it's just a small amount, and we don't know if they've got a new crop that they are cutting and bagging, so could be that the worst case is that all there is to steal is a bunch of trees, which might be hard for Bruce to hustle out."

"He wouldn't be going alone," I said.

"I dunno, Mikey," Sam said. "You get caught walking out of that house holding a bunch of trees, that's not something you can easily talk your way out of if the nosy neighbors get the law involved. Last thing you need is to get picked up by the police."

"I can think of worse things," I said.

"You don't want to be locked in one place for too long," Sam said.

"Well, that's true," I said. "Besides, I thought Fiona might enjoy this."

"There is no 'might,'" Fiona said. "I will enjoy this. Provided you don't slow me down, Bruce."

She gave him one of those looks that makes men do stupid things in hopes of seeing it again, maybe with fewer clothes involved. Bruce, naturally, had no chance with Fiona, but then very few people did.

I'd seen that look a few times. Never regretted the outcome. Too much, anyway.

"What if there is a new crop?" Bruce said.

"You don't need to take all of it," I said. "Just enough to make the Banshees angry."

"How will they know who they are mad at?" he asked.

"I've got that worked out," I said and told him what our plan was. All the Banshees would need to see was a single Ghoul patch left on the floor. No one had access to Ghoul colors but the Ghouls; or at least that was the case prior to Bruce Grossman's booty. Fiona and Bruce would leave just enough evidence to point the Banshees in the right direction. And then we'd do the rest.

"What if this doesn't work?" Bruce asked.

"That's not a possibility," I said.

"You can say that," he said, "but you'll pardon me for saying that I've never done a job with a partner before. You want me to break into the place without ever having seen it. I normally spend a few days, maybe a week, making sure I know every angle. How much time do we have for this?"

I looked at my watch. "None," I said. "We case it now. Then we make our move."

"I don't get it," he said. "How can you be sure the Banshees will be out of the house? And what about the neighbors? Have you thought any of this through?"

When you're a spy, sometimes the best way to explain a complex plan is to lie. It saves everyone a lot of worrying and heartache.

"It's all taken care of," I said. "We've actually been planning this for months, Bruce. Really. Since long before you came on the scene."

"Really?" he said. He looked to all of us and we all nodded.

Yes.

Sure.

Absolutely.

It didn't matter, really. Bruce wanted to hear the positive responses because he wanted to do the job. The only thing that could dissuade him would be if I told him it was going to end with him in a body bag. Bruce was a good bank robber, but he wasn't a "please go on without me, I'll just die right here" kind of guy.

"Okay, then, I guess I'll have to put my trust in you, Michael. And Fiona," he said. "I trust you, Fiona." Bruce gave Fi a smile that was probably very enticing over at Sherman's Deli but didn't do much for women under seventy.

"Okay," I said. "You agree to this, then you're agreeing to Sam making a few calls to see what can be done for you. There's no guarantee. If the feds don't want you, your friend Barry is going to have to find you a new life. Either way, your time as Bruce Grossman is done. Understand?"

"Being Bruce Grossman was never that great, honestly," he said. He looked down at his hand, at his missing finger, and shook his head. "You know, if I had to do it all over again, I think I would have made a pretty good spy. What do you think, Michael?"

"Maybe something a little less interactive," I said.

He chuckled. "Hmm, maybe so. You know what I might like to do in this new life? Maybe get a wife and settle down. After my mom is all taken care of, of course. Get a house in Big Sur. Maybe have a couple dogs or chickens or hamsters, you know? Something I have to take care of that I can't mess up too badly. That sounds like a good life, you ask me."

"Maybe take Maria with you," I said. The girl was listening to Bruce prattle on, but didn't seem upset. She had her own dreams, some of which the Ghouls had frightened right out of her.

"Naw," she said, "I just wanna go home. But Bruce, you got the idea. Nicky? He never had no idea what he was gonna do. But you seem like a better guy. Head screwed on, but screwed on right."

Sometimes the people you least expect to have insight are the ones who deliver the most unvarnished truth.

"We're good, then?" I said. Bruce said that we were. "Sam," I said, "why don't you see if anyone might be interested in the whereabouts of a master criminal with a fascinating insight into the mind-set of bad guys the world over."

"Will do, Mikey," Sam said and gave Bruce a big pat on the back, the special code between men that actually means "please leave so we can talk about you," which fortunately Bruce wasn't aware of and thus took the pat to mean we were all part of a big team and thus walked off with a nice stride of confidence. Nevertheless, Sam, Fiona and I walked outside and stood on the front lawn to continue our conversation.

"Nice smile you gave old Brucey there, Fiona," Sam said. "He'll be on blood thinners by the morning."

"We all have unique skills that help people acquiesce. It's not my fault that I was born with unbelievable charm."

"We're going to need more than Fi's charm to get Bruce FBI protection," Sam said.

"There's a hit squad looking for him," I said. "Shouldn't that be enough?"

"The fed boys didn't even respond to him dropping off the Ghouls' papers. He was a big deal twelve years ago, but times change, Mikey. Unless someone in the Ghouls was born in Qatar, that's back-burner stuff. He's not the asset he was."

"So make him sound better," I said.

"How am I going to do that?"

"Don't you have any friends who could, say, *improve* his sheet? Make it look like he was suspected of even more than he actually has copped to?"

"I could talk to some people," Sam said.

"Unsolved bank heists in foreign countries would be good," I said.

"What about I get him implicated in fixing *American Idol*, too?"

"Whatever it takes," I said. "I'm going to call Barry and see what we can cook up."

Ten minutes and fifteen phone numbers later, I reached Barry.

"Michael," he said, "good to hear from you." In the background I heard birdsong. Pleasant.

"Sorry to interrupt your vacation," I said.

"No worries," he said. "Did you know North Dakota is officially the friendliest state in the country?"

"That's great," I said.

"Not the best-looking people," he said, "but you make concessions when your life is at risk. They also eat everything with a cup of melted butter as a dipping sauce."

"I need your help," I said.

"I was afraid of that."

"Your friend Bruce Grossman might need a new life," I said. "We're trying to get him a little insurance."

"I thought that's what you nice government people did for a living."

"I'm not the FDIC," I said. "And besides, he's your friend, remember?"

"Right, right," Barry said. "I'm just used to playing hard to get."

"Endearing," I said. "I take it you can handle your business from North Dakota?"

"If Lewis and Clark could, I can," Barry said. "Did you know that they wintered in North Dakota? True story."

"That's great. Here's what I need: You need to build an identity for Bruce and Zadie. Good stuff. Passports that can get them into somewhere nice with good medical care."

"I can't just materialize that," Barry said. "You realize that?"

"Barry," I said, "it's either that or one day Zadie goes for therapy and comes out to some lead-pipe hitters. We're working our end tonight, but I need to know there's an out."

"I can get decent stuff," Barry said, "but we're not talking about documents that can get them into Europe. Maybe South America. But even then, it won't be permanent good."

This was not good.

"Where are you?" I said.

"A safe location."

"Specifically, Barry. This is important."

"Valley City. Sign says it's the City of Bridges."

"What are the banks like there?"

"Nice. Filled with money."

"Old or new?"

Barry paused, figuring out what I was moving toward. "You want me to check the safe-deposit boxes?"

"If you have the chance."

"Anything else?"

"Yeah," I said, "rent an apartment. A nice one."

"You'll be surprised to know that Valley City isn't exactly brimming with high-end condo complexes."

"Rent a house, then," I said. "Something big and near a hospital."

"Anything else?" Barry asked.

"A bank account," I said. "Fill it appropriately."

"This part of your fee?"

"No," I said, "this is part of you making sure your friend Bruce Grossman and his mother have a way out that does not include summering in Mozambique."

"You put it like that . . ." Barry said.

"When can you get this done?"

"I'll have it in place tonight. How will I know if it's on?"

"If you don't hear from me after midnight," I said, "don't come back to Miami."

"I love working with you, Mike," Barry said and hung up.

18

Even in the face of a natural disaster—like, say, Hurricane Katrina—people still cling to the belief that they alone can stop Mother Nature and, in the process, save their homes. Looked at unemotionally, it seems silly: Your life for wood, drywall, and furniture? But people tend to form bonds with places, to the point that it's nearly impossible to separate a person from their possessions.

So if you absolutely must get people to leave their homes, you have to make it seem like their possessions are actively causing the problems.

Most people don't know anything about their homes. Oh, they know the address. They know which bedroom is drafty in the winter, which is broiling in the summer; they know that the microwave takes thirty second to melt butter and ten seconds to warm up pie; they might even know how to turn off their gas in the event of a leak.

What they don't know, however, is what they cannot see or choose to avoid . . . which is why I went door-to-door in the cul-de-sac where the Banshees' weed farm was located to let people know that there was noxious fungus growing underneath their over-mortgaged dream homes. In order to appear to be an absolute authority on the topic, Sam and I rolled up in front of the homes in a white van. A van and a clipboard could get you into the Kremlin at the height of Communism.

"Noxious?" the man who answered the door at the house next door to the Banshees' said.

"Yup. Yup," I said. I possessed two things at that moment meant to instill perfect confidence in this fine gentleman: I was holding a clipboard and I had on a denim shirt. I also had a red bandanna in my hand and every few seconds I used it to wipe off my forehead. "And flammable, too."

"Flammable?" The man was horrified.

"Yeah, seems like it's one of those funguses that feeds off of water-based paints. You probably been reading about that? Yeah, see, what had happened is that, you know, back further on in the day when people didn't care so much about the environment, well, they just dumped their used paint into the gutter. Come to find, ten years later, that stuff is coming to roost. House on Fisher Island blew just this morning."

"Oh, my," the man said. "Well, how much time do I have to gather my belongings?"

"None," I said. "We found a fester under this street. We gotta get all of you out so we can get a hazmat team

down there to spray it all with one of those secret government potions."

"I have a dog. Can I grab my dog?"

"Yeah, old Fido is probably more susceptible, actually. I'd get him out in the next ten minutes there,
buddy."

"Why wasn't this on television?" he said. It was a
good question for him to ask. He should have asked it
about five questions previous.

"Sir, we can't have a pandemic on our hands. We
start telling people there's a fungus-humongous growing in the ground that will blow them up, we'll have
widespread panic. National Guard would get called
out. It would just be like giving Al Qaida a blueprint
on terror, you know?"

There was no color left in the man's face five minutes later when he came running out of his house—
a barking Maltese under one arm, a laptop under the
other. On the corner, Sam ushered a family of five out
of a cream-colored split-level.

That left just one more house on the cul-de-sac to
evacuate: the Banshees' smartly appointed factory.
Over the course of the last twenty minutes, while Sam
and I flushed out the other six families found on Me-
Laina Court, I kept my eye on the house for any activity. I saw nothing. The same Volvo SUV that was
depicted in the photo Sam pulled up on his computer
was parked in the driveway, but oddly there wasn't a
drip of oil to be found beneath it on the pavement.

I walked up behind the car and acted very interested in my clipboard while I took a basic inventory of what was known.

The back window of the Volvo SUV was covered in stickers. OBAMA FOR PRESIDENT. MY SON IS AN HONOR STUDENT AT CASTLE ROCK ELEMENTARY. MIAMI DOLPHINS. WE LOVE OUR COCKER! All innocuous enough, except that the window was caked with dirt and the stickers were pulled away from the window.

Inside the Volvo?

Nothing.

Not a scrap of paper.

Not a bottle of water.

Not a toy or a patch of fabric pulled up by the beloved Cocker.

I knelt down to tie my shoe and to see the underside of the carriage.

The SUV had a lattice of thin metal cable running in between all of the tires, in effect locking the car in place. If you tried to tow the car, you'd need a flatbed truck and special equipment—in short, you'd need to make a production of the event, which would provide the homeowner plenty of time to take note of the activity.

If you want to keep law enforcement from sending a battering ram into your garage, park an immobile 4,500-pound block of metal directly in front of the garage door.

Better yet, rig it with explosives. The Banshees did that, too. There was a bundle of C-4 between the two back tires. There was a bundle between the two front tires. There was also a bundle under both passenger doors.

The gases in C-4, when they explode, expand at over 26,000 feet per second. One pound of C-4 would be enough to blow up just the SUV and kill anyone within fifty feet.

There were at least twenty-five pounds of C-4 rigged to the SUV, or enough to take out the house, the truck and the rest of the cul-de-sac, leaving just a steaming crater behind.

The Banshees clearly understood the value of their property. If they'd put that much C-4 on the SUV, what was the inside of the house like?

I walked up to the front door and rang the doorbell. I listened for an echo, but instead the bell was muted inside the house. Even from just outside the door, I could feel the electric energy from inside. There was a discernible *hum* coming from just beyond the portico where I stood. I waited, and when nothing happened after a few minutes I rang the bell again.

This time I heard the sound of someone walking. The shutters beside the door opened and I made out a man's face. I waved at him and smiled. Just a guy on your porch to tell you that fungus is going to explode under your house. The shutters closed and a moment later that door cracked open.

"I don't want whatever you're selling," the man behind the door said.

"Not selling. Just telling. We got a situation involving noxious—" Before I could finish, the door slammed shut.

I rang the bell again. It opened just a crack again. "You know how to take a hint?" the man said.

I couldn't make out the man's face, but his voice made him sound like maybe he was missing something crucial, like, say, initiative.

Drive.

Will.

It's the sort of lazy drawl that creeps into common intonation when you tend to get high from your own supply.

I wedged my foot between the door and the frame and then pushed the door open a few feet. The man didn't even say anything. He just looked at my foot as if it were an interesting bug or a colorful leaf. Surprisingly, the man didn't look anything like a biker. He was maybe twenty-five, wore a plain white T-shirt and tan cargo shorts, and had on a pair of Crocs. He looked like he could be sitting in a lecture hall at UC Santa Cruz learning about the fascinating sex life of the tsetse fly.

"You gotta get out of here," he said. "This is private property."

"Sir," I said, "look around. We've evacuated all of your neighbors. There's a noxious fungus growing beneath your house. You don't get outta here, you could die. We need you out of this house in ten minutes."

The man cocked his head slightly, like he was figuring out an equation. "That doesn't make any sense," he said.

I checked my clipboard, flipped over a couple of pages, and then took a pencil from behind my ear and started scratching out some notes.

If you want someone to fear you, take notes in their presence. If you want someone to fear you who might be naturally paranoid due to an overconsumption of marijuana, take notes and ignore the person completely.

"What are you writing there?" he said. I didn't reply. "You can't take notes about me. That's against the law. You can't just start falsely recording my words, man. You hear me?"

Nothing.

"Look," he said. "I don't even live here. I'm just watching the place for some friends. I can't just leave the house. I promised them I'd stay until they got back. They got, uh, valuable stuff and things and stuff here. You know?"

I looked up from my clipboard. "I'm just noting your refusal to leave here on the form. When the fungus catches fire—did I mention the fungus is flammable?—the state isn't responsible for any loss of life. So if you're gonna stay, maybe let any pets out before they get cooked."

The man stared at me, his mouth slightly agape. It was more than he could take in at one time, apparently.

"Nine minutes," I said. "That's how long you've got now."

"Man, you don't understand," he said. "The people I work for will be pissed if I leave. Pissed like they will beat me to death pissed. These aren't nice people."

"Then why do you work for them?"

"Man, I ask myself that all the time. What I think? My dad was not a big part in my life. All I can figure."

I looked over my shoulder. Sam stood behind the Volvo with his arms crossed. He was smiling, which told me he appreciated the fine workmanship that went into rigging that SUV up to take out most of the block.

"What's your name, son?" I said.

He shifted from foot to foot, like maybe he had to pee but didn't want to tell his dad. "Max Yennie," he said. "Are you going to write that down?"

"No, Max," I said.

"Good, I mean, because this shit here, man, it's not permanent. It's, like, my passion, but not my permanent passion. Does that make sense?"

"Eight minutes," I said.

Max Yennie looked into the house and then back at me. "This fungus, it won't blow up the house if I get out in eight minutes?"

"It won't blow up if we are able to get underground and stop it, in seven and a half minutes now."

"See, the thing is—" He started rambling on about the government and about legalization of drugs and about his dad, so I did the only thing I could to close this situation out in a timely fashion: I hit Max Yennie in the face. I grabbed him on the way down and brought him to the floor lightly so he wouldn't blow out his knee. I punched Max in the chin, not hard enough to do any permanent damage but just enough to keep him out for long enough to get him away from the house.

I waved Sam up to the door.

"You perceive a clear and present danger here with Spicoli?" Sam asked.

"He wouldn't stop talking long enough for me to convince him to get out," I said. "Evasive action needed to be taken."

"What are we gonna do with him? Your mom's house is getting a little crowded."

"Let's drag him inside and tie him up. We'll figure it out from there. Where's Bruce?"

"They're parked about two miles away," Sam said. "I gotta tell you, Mikey, Fiona is slightly agitated."

"How can you tell?"

"She texted me. She said she was slightly agitated. Apparently Bruce keeps asking her out for dinner. She's thinking she might drive him off of a pier if things turn out adversely."

"I thought she wanted to pick his brain," I said. "She should be enjoying this quiet time with him."

We gathered up Max Yennie and tied his hands behind his back with his own belt. It was made from hemp, so it had nice strength. We needed to get him out of the way so that when Bruce and Fiona "broke into" the house, he wouldn't pose a problem. It would have been easier for me to run in and do the job myself, but in order for us to get Bruce aboard—really, to save him from himself—I needed to have him feel like he was the mastermind of a great crime. Having Fiona help him was just a bit of sugar; something he could hold on to in the future when he was working with suits on issues related to bank security.

Or that was the plan provided Sam ever heard back from his buddies in the Bureau. If he didn't hear back from them, we'd need Barry's help. "Bring the van around," I said to Sam once we had Max restrained appropriately. "Let's get this guy out of sight."

While Sam got the van, I took a look inside the house. The entryway was nicely tiled and the living room looked like it had been cut and pasted from a Pottery Barn catalog. But one thing you can't hide with nice tile and furniture is the smell of an entire forest of marijuana being cultivated inside of a house, particularly since the temperature in the house was at least eighty-five degrees, which gave everything a dank, swampy feel.

I opened a door at the end of the entry hall and found what used to be a kitchen. There was still plenty of counter space and a nice sink in place, but the flooring had been ripped out and a series of tubes and cables crisscrossed the place where the floor used to be. Water sprayed periodically into the air from one of the tubes and a whirring overhead fan spun lazily. For a moment I was reminded of Havana, until I remembered that when I was in Havana I never saw ten-foot-high marijuana trees inside a $500,000 house.

I heard a sound behind me and saw that Max was starting to stir. I would need to handle this situation delicately. I knelt down in front of him.

"Max," I said, "you've been hit in the face."

"My jaw really hurts," he said.

"It's going to for about a week. You might want to see a dentist if your bite feels off."

Max processed that. "You're not here to kill me?"

"No," I said, "but I am going to need to kidnap you for a little while. When we release you, I'd advise you to find another line of work. Because eventually? Your bosses would find a reason to kill you and that's no kind of job security."

"Yeah," Max said. "The economy, man, you know."

"I know," I said. Sam pulled the van around, so I stood Max up and walked him outside. We put him in the back of the van, which didn't seem to bother him, since he just kept jabbering on.

"Should I duct-tape his mouth?" Sam said.

I thought for a moment. "No," I said, "let's see if we can find him some pork rinds."

"Good plan," Sam said and closed the door on Max.

After we got the van moving, I called Fiona. "You ready?" I asked when she picked up.

"What am I doing again?"

"You're indulging a fantasy," I said. "And probably saving a life."

"And what do I earn on this?"

"Steal whatever you like," I said.

"No one to beat up, then?"

"I think you've done enough."

"I just assumed there'd be some terribly scarred and intermittently stoned caretaker I could engage."

"No, I took care of that," I said. "The house is empty. The street is vacant for at least thirty minutes, so get in and out and make as big a mess as possible."

"Yes, about that." Fiona lowered her voice. "Bruce wants to break in through the roof."

"So break in through the roof," I said.

"Michael, I don't want him falling on me," she whispered.

"The front door is open," I said. "Tell him to check it first and then get in and out."

"That's a plan I can support," she said, a hint of mischief in her voice. Happy again. Nothing like the freedom to do a rush bang-and-run job to get Fiona off the bubble.

"Just make sure to leave enough evidence," I said.

"Michael, if Bruce keeps hitting on me, I might leave a body," she said. "Anything else?"

"Don't touch the SUV in the driveway," I said. "It's wired with enough C-4 to take out the eastern seaboard."

"Nice touch."

"And if any soccer moms return to their homes early, try not to do anything that might accidentally send the SUV up in flames. Or any of their SUVs."

It's not that I think Fiona would actually do these things. Rather, it's important to point out to her that I know she's capable of doing these things, which will put the seed in her head, true, but will also remind her that she's not allowed to blow up everything in the vicinity. These days, with no one protecting me and no one protecting Fiona but me, it's wise to keep a buffer between myself and wholesale destruction.

"You are the enemy of fun," Fiona said. "Would you like to speak with Robin Hood before we initiate our crime spree?"

"No," I said.

"Great, here he is," Fiona said and then Bruce said, "Hey, buddy. This is going to work great."

"Fantastic," I said.

"I'll show our little Irish friend a trick or two."

"You do that."

"And Michael?"

"Yes, Bruce?"

"Thank you," he said. "For all of this: I'm an old man. And I know that."

"You're welcome," I said and meant it.

"If something happens to me," he said, "you'll take care of my mother?"

"Nothing is going to happen to you," I said.

"But if something did."

Working with clients is often more about human resources management than actual hand-to-hand fighting or innovative spying technology. People, at the end of the day, want to be protected and want their families to be protected. Bruce, on the other hand, had already done the most he could to try to keep his mother safe, had sacrificed time—years, really—a finger, and was willing to commit a crime against a gang of men who'd just as soon kill themselves as let him walk the earth knowing he'd gotten over on them.

It wasn't guts, exactly.

It wasn't heroism.

It was probably a lot like love.

We do things for our parents because even if we have issues with them, there's a genetic responsibility. There's a reason I fixed up the Charger and there's a reason I've fixed my mother's disposal ten times in the last eighteen months.

"If a tsunami rolls into Miami," I said, "or a hurricane or a plague of locusts or every motorcycle gang in the country, know that all of them will need to go through me to get to your mother. And then Fiona, too."

"Really?"

"Really," I said.

"Okay, then," he said. He gave the phone back to Fiona.

"All taken care of," I said.

"Wonderful," Fiona said and then, in the background, I heard Bruce shout, "Let's do some crime, little lady!"

19

If you really want to violate someone, to make them feel afraid and lost and vulnerable, steal something from them that appears to have zero street value. Stealing a computer or a television or a car is an understandable crime—there's a tangible reward along the line. But if you steal someone's shoes, or their photo album, or a single candlestick, the person you steal it from is going to have complex emotions of loss coupled with the sense that their lives are somehow being perpetually invaded.

Which is why Fiona stole all of the Banshees' C-4 from beneath the SUV.

And the steering wheel from the SUV.

And the Obama sticker.

And destroyed the hydroponic system in the kitchen and set off a fire extinguisher in the upstairs bedrooms, which is where packages of marijuana were being packed and readied for shipment.

So while Bruce carted away enough marijuana to start his own summer reggae tour—which he and

Fiona then promptly dumped into a canal—Fiona carted away the security the Banshees had.

Not only had they been robbed.

Not only was their man of the house missing.

Not only had their means of continued production been destroyed.

On top of all of that, they also had been made to look weak and foolish.

And the Ghouls had done it.

Or, well, that's what they clearly understood the situation to be, which we overheard since Fiona left a bug in the house, too, which was helpful. After taking Bruce back to my mother's, the three of us—Sam, Fi and I—listened to the recording from the bug while eating a healthy snack of multiflavored yogurts in my loft.

The Banshees sounded, not too surprisingly, a little on the salty side of things.

"I don't know if what that guy called the Ghouls is anatomically possible," Sam said.

"You should learn how to stretch your back muscles," Fi said.

"I stretch them plenty," Sam said. "Carrying Michael around takes a lot of strength, Fiona, don't kid yourself."

I took a bite of my yogurt and tried to concentrate on the men, not on the warring factions of Sam and Fiona. Fi and Bruce had done an excellent job destroying the house and what they stole—including the C-4—indicated a desire not just to rip off the

Banshees but to humiliate them, to show them that not only were they weak, but they were vulnerable. And instead of leaving a loose patch—one that maybe had been inadvertently torn from clothing while destroying the house, Fiona took it one step further: she burned the word "Ghouls" into the nice manicured lawn in the backyard.

Give Fiona thirty minutes and she'll give you wholesale destruction of real property.

The Banshees were mad. They wanted revenge.

Things were finally—finally—falling into place.

"What he just said, about the lead pipe? That's not possible unless you're in zero gravity," Sam said and then his cell phone rang. We'd been waiting all day to hear back from the feds, see if they'd take Bruce and his mother in.

"That them?" I asked.

"Looks like it," he said and answered it. He mumbled a few words, nodded his head, suggested that the person on the other end of the phone line might, in fact, want to try out a zero-gravity chamber sometime in the near future, and bring a lead pipe with them, and then clicked his phone off.

"No dice," he said.

"Yeah, I got that."

"I tried making his file look better, even tied him into a bank job in Manila in the early nineties, but it seems like it would have been impossible for him to be there."

"You don't say."

"I do say," Sam said. "Apparently he was in court that day. In Michigan. As a juror."

"If he wasn't smart enough to get out of jury duty," Fiona said, "why on earth would your government want to help him?"

"Well, that and the recession. My guy tells me that Witness Protection spending got cut in half, so they're only taking people who really need protecting. You know, like those Bear Stearns people. Looks like it's on Barry to set him up."

This wasn't the best result. But we could make it work. What I knew was that in order to get Bruce to go along quietly, to not rob any more places, to actually go on his own accord to North Dakota, we'd need to convince him he was going under protection.

Fortunately, he had a bit of money and Barry could get him more, plus a North Dakota–good identity. He would need to stay there at least until all the Ghouls in Miami were somewhere else. Even still, we'd give them back their treasured paper and fabric. All of this for paper and fabric.

In the meantime, we had to make sure that the Ghouls and the Banshees met somewhere in the middle of this action, so that they might just cancel each other out. Or, better yet, find themselves locked up for several years—enough time to get Zadie set up in permanent care and Bruce in a place where he couldn't hurt himself.

So while Sam and Fiona continued listening to the bug, I called Barry and told him what he needed to know.

"Complicated," Barry said.

"Busy week, Barry," I said.

"Mike, Valley City is a very calming place," he said. "Maybe you and Fiona should rent a cabin here and rekindle the passion when this is all through."

"What would we do with Sam?"

"They have a place here called Shake's Bar and Grill. They have hot peanuts and cold beers. He'd make do."

"I'll have my assistant get on that," I said. "Where are you with the plan?"

"A lovely Craftsman came available today," he said. "Only cost me five thousand to get the tenants out, another five thousand to get them to Hawaii."

"Real money?"

"Mike, it's North Dakota."

"Right. Okay, it looks like Bruce and his mother are on the way. I'll let you know for sure soon. There any chance you know any dependable muscle in that part of the country?"

"I got some favors I could call in," he said. "Might cost a bit."

"Barry," I said, "you're the client. Remember?"

"This is odd for me."

"I know, we'll work through it. In the meantime, I need guys who wear suits," I said. "Maybe ex-feds who now use their powers for evil. Know anyone like that?"

"I only know you and Sam," he said. "What about ex–Coast Guard? Miami is filled with ex–Coast Guard."

"Just a few guys who can sit behind the wheel of an American car in front of the Craftsman periodically. Let Bruce and Zadie know they are being watched, but in a good way."

Barry made a noise into the phone that sounded a lot like a painful groan. As if maybe he were having a root canal without Novocaine.

"You okay?" I asked.

"Just thinking about the cost," he said. "How do people afford all of this? Isn't it easier to just go to the police?"

"Yes," I said. "You should do that."

Barry groaned again. "I see the fly in the ointment here," he said.

"That's the problem with being a criminal, Barry. You just can't turn to the police when you really need to."

"You know, Mike, I didn't realize this was going to become an international incident. I would have just booked a cruise for Bruce and his mom if I had—one of those Alaskan ones? You know where you're on board for a month and you tour icebergs?"

"It's all right," I said. "These things happen when you're a small-business owner."

"I know," he said, "I'm just trying to make it clear to you that getting me involved in something this large as payback would be, you know, within reason. I'm just not looking forward to the part where some Cold War relic comes searching for you and decides to take me out first to send a message. I've seen that before."

"You have?"

"Get cable, Mike," Barry said. "You'll learn a lot."

I told Barry he'd hear from me shortly, to stay by one of his fifteen phones and be prepared to possibly book a charter flight out of Miami. This news did not make him happy, either.

I hung up with Barry and briefed Sam and Fi. "Next time you speak to Barry," Fi said, "let him know I could use a few ex–Coast Guard boys, too. I have a couple of shipments coming into town that they might be just right for. Grenade launchers can be very cumbersome to carry."

"Cubans again?" Sam said.

"Maybe," she said. "Or maybe I'll just keep them for July Fourth."

I tried to steer the conversation back toward something near productivity. "What else did you guys pick up on the bug?"

"Banshees are ready to move," Sam said. "They just don't know where to hit."

"Maybe we should show them," I said.

"I don't know how fast those bikes we have are," Sam said. "They growl and they look nice, but if I'm

being chased by a hundred angry bikers, I'd like to
have some extra juice."

"How long would it take you to install a new power
tube and ignition?" I asked.

"Couple hours, give or take," he said.

"Before midnight?"

"If it's the difference between being fast and being
slow?" he said. He reached for a pencil and made some
calculations on a scrap of paper. "Says here a six-pack
of Corona and some limes and a nice wrench set will
assure that the bikes are tricked out by eleven."

I reached into my pocket and pulled out my wallet, gave Sam whatever I had—somewhere around five
hundred bucks, the last of the cash Barry gave me to
front this job—and then watched Sam leave the loft.
He was somewhere between giddy and joyous. Hard
to tell the difference in a man like Sam, but I had a feeling that the money I gave him would cover the parts,
the six-pack and probably another six-pack or four.

That left Fiona and me alone. There'd been something brewing between us these last few days—not
exactly flirting, because Fiona was constantly flirting,
but just a reminder that there existed a bright aura of
availability.

"You ready?" I said.

"James Bond could get a jet pack and anti-shark
repellent in less than hour," Fiona said. She'd settled
down onto my bed with another cup of yogurt, though
she was eating it with some apparent distaste. She was

much more of a carnivore. "And here you are, eleventh hour, sending Sam out for parts."

"And beer."

"James Bond would have us drinking martinis."

"You fell for the wrong spy," I said.

"Pushed," she said. "Led by unseen forces beyond my control."

I sat down beside her on the bed. I wasn't sure why. But things were feeling . . . positive.

And then the phone rang.

"Michael," my mother said when I picked it up, "there's a man with a beard standing across the street."

"They're back in fashion," I said. I was still leaning in toward Fiona, things still seemed like they might well work in a direction I could be comfortable with, at least until I became uncomfortable and even that would be okay, I supposed . . .

"There's another one standing next to him holding a bat. They look like Laurel and Hardy."

. . . and then I was bolt upright.

The Glucks.

Something, somewhere, had gone wrong in the plan.

"Where's Nate?" I said. I went to the kitchen and grabbed my gun. And then another gun. And then one more. Fiona didn't know what was happening, but she took my aggressive arming as a sign and did likewise. She now looked palpably more excited than she had when it appeared I was about to kiss her.

"He's taking a nap. He's had an exhausting day taking Zadie back and forth to appointments, so I didn't want to bother him. But he and Maria seem to be getting along very well. She might be a nice girl for him, Michael. Like Fiona could have been if you hadn't messed that up."

"Mom," I said, as calmly as possible, "wake Nate up and tell him to secure the house. He'll know what to do."

I didn't actually know if this was true, but it would take me ten minutes to get home and with what we already had in place surrounding the house, all Nate really needed to do was turn off HGTV, close the shutters and make sure he had plenty of bullets nearby.

"What about me?" she asked.

"Grab your shotgun and stay low," I said.

There was a pause. This was not a time for pauses.

"Where's your shotgun, Ma?"

"In the car with Bruce."

No.

No.

No.

This was not happening.

We were already out of the loft, running down the stairs. The bikes were there, as was the Charger. I wasn't looking especially biker-ish in my worker uniform anymore, so I didn't bother with the artifice. At some point, disguises and poses and your ability to sidle up to someone become irrelevant.

In those cases, a bad man with a bad woman, armed to the teeth with automatic weapons and driving a 1974 Charger usually suffices.

"Where is Bruce?"

"Don't use that patronizing tone, Michael. He's an adult."

"Ma," I said, "those two men out in front of the house are there to kill Bruce. They are also there to probably kill me. The odds are fair that if they see you first, they'll kill you, too, so pretty please, with sugar plum fairies, tell me where Bruce went."

"He ran out to get us all some dinner. He said he had steaks in his freezer at home."

I pressed down on the gas and the Charger lunged forward. "I will be there in seven minutes," I said. "If those two men get any closer to the house, shoot them." I hung up and called Sam. "Change to the itinerary," I told him. "The Ghouls are staking out my mother's house."

"That's not good, Mikey."

"Understatement," I said. We came to a stoplight and, after safely checking both directions of oncoming traffic, and properly flashing my lights and honking the horn . . . I blew through it going about ninety-five. Beside me, Fiona was loading guns and strapping knives to herself, which, while hot, would not be a great experience if we happened to get sideswiped.

Or pulled over by a cop.

Like the one I didn't see hiding behind a parked RV

until I was already fifty yards beyond him and screaming toward my mother's house.

His lights immediately went on, as did the blaring siren.

"Do I hear a siren?" Sam said.

"No," I said.

"That's good," Sam said. "Because for a minute I thought maybe highway patrol was chasing you."

"It's actually a siren *and* a horn you hear," I said. I looked in the rearview mirror. "And he looks like a regular traffic cop."

"That's a relief," Sam said. "You have some direction for me, Mikey?"

"One moment please," I said. We were approaching a school zone and even though it was early evening, police tend to hang out near school zones to pick up speeders. And drug dealers. And gangbangers. And if they got lucky today, they'd get a former bank robber for the IRA who now sold guns to Cuban revolutionaries and a burned spy, both of whom had enough artillery on them to take down Guam in a bloody coup.

The motorcycle cop was still behind me and by that point was probably actively working the radio. If it was a slow crime day, they'd probably scramble a helicopter, which would then get the news helicopters in the air, which would then get all of this on the news.

This could work to my advantage, so I gunned the Charger through the school zone, my own horn honking, my own lights blinking, trying to get as much attention as possible.

"Bruce is either dead or hiding somewhere near my mother's, so I need you to drag the Banshees there."

"I'm not sure if the rental van can outrun a bunch of hogs," Sam said.

In my rearview mirror, I could see the motorcycle cop gaining on me. He wasn't close enough to see my plate and we hadn't traveled far enough for this to be considered a high-speed chase, because a reasonable lawyer could conjecture that while the cop was on my tail, I was driving so recklessly as to not notice. Plus, I was driving fairly conservatively, if incredibly fast. Safety first and all that.

"You have to try," I said. "How close are you to the weed house?"

"I can be there in five minutes," he said.

"When you get there," I said, "shoot it up. Maybe take out the SUV, make a big bang, big enough that they'll follow you quick."

"You sure Fiona got all the C-4?" Sam asked. "I'd rather not add a meteor crater to the list of Miami's attractions."

I turned to Fiona—she was quietly sharpening a knife against a mortarboard, as calm and detached as if she were doing her nails (while driving ninety-five miles per hour with the cops on her tail). "All of the C-4 is out of the SUV, right?"

Fiona lifted one shoulder.

"Yes or no, Fi, because Sam is going to blow it up in about three minutes."

"I guess he'll know when he blows it up," she said. "I'd advise him to stand at least one foot from any open flame."

"Sam," I said, "do the drive-by like the kids do these days. No stopping to admire. But hang back enough for the Banshees to see you. We need to draw them out right now and get them heading toward my mother's."

"On it," he said and hung up.

As soon as the phone was off, it rang.

Nate.

I handed the phone to Fiona. "Would you mind taking a message?" I said. "I need to not accidentally kill anyone."

"You really need to get a Bluetooth," Fiona said. "It's very dangerous to talk on the phone while driving."

We flew through an intersection just as another motorcycle cop came peeling into view.

We were now being chased.

This would take some explaining, but that was fine. I'd be happy to explain that I was coming to help my mother, who apparently was being held hostage by a brimming motorcycle gang turf war.

Provided I could get to the house before shots started getting fired.

Fiona answered the phone, said a few words, and then dropped it in my lap. "It's your brother," she said.

Sometimes Fiona is difficult just to be difficult. It suits her, but it's not always an enjoyable aspect of her personality.

"Nate," I said, just as we passed a Starbucks that used to be a coin-op laundry Nate and I used to steal quarters from (a knife, a paper clip and a can of WD-40 were all you needed to pry open the coin depository on the old washers). "I can't really talk. I'm being chased by the police."

"Yeah," he said, "I hear a bunch of sirens. That you?"

"I'm about half a mile away," I said, "coming from the east. That where the sound is coming from?"

"Actually, it's coming from all over. In stereo, pretty much."

"Good," I said.

"Yeah," he said.

"Is there something you wanted to talk about, Nate, or can this wait until after I'm done evading capture?"

"I just wanted to apologize," he said. "I think these guys found the house because of me."

"Why is that, Nate?"

I turned left, which was technically away from the house, but I wanted to get a sense of how many police were potentially following me. I knew of two at least, but hadn't seen any air support.

I used my blinker.

My seat belt was on, and apart from the cache of guns in the car, I was really only guilty of speeding at this point.

And failure to yield.

And some red light problems.

But I was thinking of killing my brother.

"I dropped Zadie off and ran a couple of errands. When I got back she said she had a really nice conversation with a young lady in leather pants about me. Zadie points her out in the parking lot, so I go over and drop a little game on her."

"Drop a little game on her?"

"I talked her up, told her I was staying out at Mom's, and, you know, to call me there. Maybe we'd get together and watch religious television together and hand-knit bedspreads. Couple hours later, I realized, you know, maybe that she was a plant."

"Maybe."

"And, well, now there's about fifteen bikers circling the house. I'm really sorry, Michael."

"How about instead of apologizing, maybe load a couple of guns?"

"Mom is on that," Nate said. "And Maria is pretty handy around a nine. Zadie's boiling water in case they break the perimeter. She said that's how we won World War One."

I looked into the rearview mirror and saw . . . nothing. I looked to my right: nothing. I looked to my left: nothing. I looked at Fiona. She'd put away all of her weapons and was now texting with someone.

And I didn't hear any sirens.

"Nate," I said, "I'll be there in two minutes. Don't

let anyone into the house. And if the cops come, stay indoors."

I pulled over at an intersection only a few blocks from my mother's.

"What are we doing?" Fi asked.

"Waiting," I said.

"Is that the best idea?"

"Do you see any police?"

Fiona did the same compass pass I'd just performed. "Where are they?" she asked.

"Listen," I said.

In the distance I could make out the faint sound of about a hundred sirens humming alongside the growling of motorcycles. There was a good chance the cop following me was called off pursuit for a larger, more dangerous issue—namely, a horde of thugs speeding through residential Miami.

I called Sam.

"ETA?" I said.

"I'll be there in about five minutes," he said. "I've got a posse on my back that you wouldn't believe."

"Any shots fired?"

"Not yet," Sam said.

"If you pass an open field, bury a bullet."

"I like that idea," Sam said.

"Tell me what street you're on," I said. He did and then I hung up with him and called 911.

"Yes, thank you, I'd like to report a very serious situation. There are approximately two hundred men on motorcycles chasing a man in a white van down Reston Avenue. One of the motorcycle people just fired a gun. Yes. Very frightening. My name?" I paused for one moment and thought it through. "Clifford Gluck," I said and then hung up.

"This is exactly how you planned it, right?" Fiona said.

"This is all contingency training, Fi," I said. "Textbook stuff."

"Funny," she said. "Oh, yes, the old pit-two-enemies-together-to-kill-each-other-off-so-a-third-party-can-prosper textbook. I heard about it on Twitter. The kids love it. Always such a winning plan."

"Vietnam?" I said.

"Yes, that ended up particularly well."

"Iraq?"

"Another solid victory for the good guys," she said.

I kept thinking and watching the intersection, waiting for the inevitable flurry of action. Two or three minutes later, it flashed by: a hunk of white followed by what looked liked a swarm of giant flies. The police were not yet on the scene, but I could already feel the ionic change in the air—a helicopter was nearby, but it was also the release of anxiety and breath and sweat by the people on the street.

When people talk about sensing fear, this is what they mean. When you're scared, your sweat emits a different smell, a genetic marker that one can pick up on and exploit. The breeze rolls by and things smell and feel different and you start to feel anxious and aware, it's usually because you're perceiving someone else's fear.

"We need to ditch some guns," I said. If I was going to show up at my mother's at the same time cops were, it would be wise not to have an arsenal of illegal guns on my person, nor would it be great if Fiona came sliding out of the Charger strapped like Bigfoot was coming after her stamp collection. A pretty face and a cute walk go a long way, but a pretty face and a cute walk and several guns in front of twitchy-fingered beat cops could mean a bullet.

And I really didn't want Fiona shooting anyone.

"Do you propose I walk into the Chick-fil-A and just hand them what I have?"

She had a point.

I looked around the area. There was indeed a Chick-fil-A, but there was also a library, a gas station and three houses. In front of one of the houses was a gutter.

"We'll dump them in the gutter," I said.

"I have to tell you that I find this offensive on every level," she said, but then she gathered up what we had, leaving us each with one gun, and threw the rest into the drain system. She got back into the car silently.

A girl separated from her guns is never a time for joy.

I started the car back up and drove at a natural rate of speed toward my mother's, though with the windows down so I could hear the sirens and any shots.

The sirens were easy enough to hear—they came in crashing waves.

And then came the gunfire—a wail of shots echoed into the air as I pulled onto the street adjacent to my mother's. It was mostly small-arms fire from what I could hear, which made sense. The gangs weren't known to be stocked with a lot of rifles and submachine guns. What was clear, however, was that there was a volley going on—an all-out assault vs. an all-out assault. You could hear the call and response of battle.

This would be good for home values in the neighborhood.

If everything was working as planned—or, at least, as recently devised—the Ghouls and the Banshees were now doing a bit of mutual assured destruction. The police would be arriving soon enough, but one thing police are keen to do is let bad guys kill bad guys. It's a lot less paperwork in the short and long term. If we got lucky, the Ghouls would be so busy with the Banshees, they'd be forced to forget about Bruce for at least a few minutes, and that meant they'd forget about my mother's house and all of the people inside.

Still, I had to be there to be sure.

I started to get out of the car, but Fiona stopped me. "You can't be seen there," she said. "You walk into the middle of that gunfight and you'll either be killed or arrested. And if you're arrested, you have no idea if you'll ever see freedom again."

She was right, but I couldn't stand by, either.

If you're a good spy, you don't need to be the instigator of violence to be effective. Sometimes it's enough just to be the guy who makes everyone else feel safer.

"I'll be fine," I said. "Take the car back to the loft. I'll call you when it's over." I leaned over and kissed her once on the cheek before jumping out of the car. I hurdled the Evanses' side fence, took the Strongs' back gate in a nice swing move, scaled the Williamses' block wall, shimmied under the Mecklenburgs' bougainvillea bush (which was just a sprig when I was a kid) and then wormed my way into my own backyard.

The sound of gunfire was intense, but the sound of approaching sirens was pervasive. I looked up and saw not one but three helicopters hovering.

The news has always loved to televise bad people doing bad things to one another, especially when they do so in unusual places, like, say, neighborhoods filled with blue light specialers.

My main goal now, however, was to navigate the labyrinth of razor wire I'd prepared in the yard, as I'd become accustomed to having two Achilles tendons and had every intention of growing old with both. I put my head down and watched every step, remembering the pattern of the wire, the circle pattern meant to ensnare even the most limber advancing army, which in this case would be me. All I knew was that I had to get into the house and make sure all was okay.

"Don't take another step or I'll blast you."

I looked up to find Zadie clutching a shotgun. She didn't have her glasses on, so I was likely just a blur moving through the yard. She was looking to her right. I was standing about twenty feet to her left.

"Zadie," I said, "it's Michael. Don't shoot." I took a step forward and she fired a single shot that conveniently found its way into the dirt about five feet behind me and to the left.

"Are you dead?" she asked.

"No, Zadie, I'm still standing right here."

"You didn't run off?"

"No, Zadie, I didn't. Now put that gun down before you hurt someone."

"You say you're Michael?"

"That's what I say, yes," I said.

"How do I know it's you?" she said.

"You could go inside and get my mother," I said. "Just don't tell her you shot at me. My mother reacts very poorly to people who try to shoot her son."

I could almost see the gears working in Zadie's head. Eventually she lowered the gun. It must have made sense to her, so I kept walking until I was directly in front of her and then gently removed the shotgun from her hands.

"Let me take that," I said.

"In my day I was a pretty good shot," she said.

"I'm sure you were," I said.

The gunfire on the street had come to a stop and now I heard the barking of police officers, shouting, screaming, moaning, and the approaching sound of more than one ambulance. I didn't know where Sam was, or his condition, only that he'd brought a war zone to bear on my mother's street and the likely result was that the bad guys were now about to be the incarcerated guys. My first concern, however, was the collateral damage.

I looked Zadie over. She was unwounded. She didn't even seem all that nervous. "Are you okay?" I said.

"This isn't the first time I've heard people fighting," she said.

"That was a bit more than a fight," I said.

"I ever tell you about my husband robbing buses?"

"Yes," I said.

"So maybe sometimes he wasn't alone."

You learn a lot about someone if you know how to get the right stories out of them.

I put my arm through Zadie's and guided her inside the house, where we found Nate crouched behind a sofa, my mother and Maria beside him. Maria's dog stood panting over them. There was no blood and it didn't look like any bullets had come sailing through the windows. I peered out the window and saw a dozen police cruisers, SWAT members, three ambulances and a lot of people on the ground.

This was going to be on the news. Probably nationally.

What I didn't see was a gold Lincoln. Lyle Connors was behind a desk somewhere following all this on his BlackBerry while sitting in a management course. A good leader has plausible deniability. A great leader has actual deniability.

I also didn't see a white van. Where was Sam?

"You can get up now," I said.

"How do you know?" Nate said.

"If you ever see more blue lights in your house than blood, you're safe."

Nate checked himself. No wounds. My mother stood up, walked into the kitchen, pulled open a drawer and a pack of cigarettes and immediately lit up. "If I'm going to die," she said, "it will be on my terms."

Maria just sat dazed next to Nate, absently petting her dog. This had not been a particularly good week in Maria's life.

"Are you all right?" I asked.

"Pretty far from that," she said. "Can I go home?"

"Soon," I said.

I looked back outside. Still no Sam, but also no Bruce. I knew Sam could take care of himself and I knew, if given a rope, Bruce had the capacity to tie his own noose. That he—or his body—wasn't outside was good. If they'd already managed to kill him, it's likely the Ghouls wouldn't have bothered with the possible slaughterhouse of an entire household in a quiet Miami neighborhood.

"Maria," I said, "do you have somewhere safe you

can go if need be? A place where your family won't be under any duress?"

"I have a cousin in Ohio," she said.

"Ohio is nice this time of year," I said.

There was a knock on the back door and then it began to open with the same perceptible creak it has had since 1981.

"Get the boiling water!" Zadie shouted.

"Easy there, Toots," came a voice, followed by the welcome vision of Sam Axe, a Stella in one hand, a gun in the other.

"Where have you been?" I asked.

"Setting the van on fire," he said.

"I thought that was a rental," I said.

"Technically, yes, it belonged to a rental company." Sam kicked off his shoes and plopped down on the sofa. "You know what I like?" he said.

"Being alive?"

"That the Banshees and Ghouls fight Civil War style. One on one side, one on the other. And then everyone goes bang-bang. John Wayne would be proud."

"Any sighting of Bruce?" I said quietly, lest Zadie start to worry.

"Nope," Sam said. "Mikey, I don't have a great feeling about this."

"No," I said. I called Fiona to tell her we, at least, were all alive.

"I know," she said.

"Where are you?"

"I ditched the car a few blocks away and am now standing at the end of the street surrounded by senior citizens in tears. Seems they never knew their neighborhood was a hotbed for criminal activity, or at least it hasn't been since those Westen boys moved away."

"Yeah," I said, "listen. There's still no sign of Bruce."

"He's a cagey one, Michael. He's probably fine."

"Keep an eye out," I said and hung up.

I checked my watch. We didn't have much time before the police would begin canvassing the neighborhood for information, which meant a bunch of people with a cache of guns and dubious backstories was not going to be good news for anyone.

"Listen up," I said. "In about ten minutes a cop is going to come to the door. Ma, I need you to collect all of the guns and put them in the laundry room. Inside the dryer and the washing machine will be fine. Put the shotgun in a closet. Maria, for the next hour, you and Nate are a couple and you've come over for lunch to meet Nate's mother. Okay?"

Maria nodded once. Nate seemed happier about this than was reasonable for the circumstances.

"Zadie, you're . . ." I paused. "Zadie, you just be yourself."

"What about me, Mike?" Sam asked.

"You're Sam Axe, friend to the helpless and downtrodden," I said.

"Got it."

I sat down next to Sam on the sofa and took a sip of his beer.

"Who are you?" he asked.

"I have no idea anymore," I said.

It took two hours, but the police eventually came by my mother's house.

"Everyone okay here?" the cop asked. He was looking at his notebook and didn't even bother to make eye contact with me.

"Fine, fine," I said. "Just ruined a nice afternoon for us is all."

"Seems like there was an explosion here a few months ago?"

"Yes," I said. By my count, there'd probably been five or six in the last two years. "Faulty wiring. You know how these old houses are."

"There a good reason there's razor wire in the bushes out front?"

"My mother's house has been egged repeatedly by neighbor kids," I said.

The cop finally looked up at me now with something close to sympathy in his eyes. "Kids can make you crazy."

"Indeed," I said.

The cop asked a couple of questions: Had we seen anything prior to the shoot-out? Did we know of any gang members who lived on the street? Had any of us seen a white van in the area?—and after we lied sufficiently, he asked if I had any questions before he left.

"Any idea why they chose here to fight?" I asked.

He turned his palms over. "Who knows, right? Stupid people do stupid things."

The cop was right, of course, but that didn't explain where Bruce Grossman was.

After the police allowed us to leave, Sam and I took Maria back to her house but told her now was the time to see what life in Ohio looked like, but to stay in contact as we still didn't know if we'd need her. The scene outside my mother's house was grisly, enough so that it seemed likely all the players involved would have much larger concerns than the fact that one guy ripped them off for money, and information, and pride.

Still, I wasn't convinced Bruce was alive. Fiona may have been correct about his cageyness, but I was more concerned with finding something concrete, so Sam and I drove back to Zadie's house to see if there was any sign of him. The house looked from the outside precisely the way we'd left it—which is to say, the glass front door was broken and inside the house, tire tracks and cat heads were everywhere.

"I'm gonna guess Zadie will want this cleaned up before she moves back in," Sam said.

"That sounds like a good way for Nate to apologize," I said.

We moved room to room, guns out, just in case someone else was there who maybe wasn't so friendly.

When we stepped into Bruce's bedroom, it was empty except for a single envelope on the floor with my name on the front.

"You think it's Dolphins season tickets?" Sam said.

I opened it up and Sam and I read the letter inside:

I wanted to say thank you for all of your help. I spoke with Barry and he's going to set up care for my mother in that place you guys talked about, too, I guess. I've spent the last 12 years in prison and I'm not about to go back to prison again, even if it's a whole state. Have you ever been to that place? It's a sweet idea, but I'm 65. I'll get the rest of my money to Barry shortly and then I'll send more when my mother needs it. I've got a couple of places I want to check out first, if you know what I mean. Thanks again and thank Fiona for making me feel alive again. Oh—one other thing: I returned all of the Ghouls' paperwork to them while they were busy plotting my death this evening. I'm good to my word, Michael, as you were to yours.

Bruce

I folded the letter in half and in half again and then ripped it into tiny pieces.

"Barry told him the truth," I said.

"Mike," Sam said, "they're friends. What did you expect?"

"This was a chance for Bruce to go completely straight," I said.

"Just like you?" Sam said. "You maybe thinking about taking a job as a security guard at a bank now? Wasn't that someone's bright idea once?"

We walked outside and stood for a moment on the front porch and just looked at the empty street. It was late and the air had turned cool. There were only a few more nights like this left before summer would make even the latest hour feel like noon.

A gold Lincoln pulled down the street then and stopped right in front of the house. The back window rolled down and Lyle Connors stared out at us. He blinked once and then stepped out of his car and walked toward us.

"Hello, Lyle," I said.

"Jasper," he said. "If that's your name."

"It isn't," I said.

Lyle ran his tongue over his lips, but he couldn't stop himself from smiling. "Fed?"

"If I were a fed," I said, "you'd be in prison. But it's early yet, so you never know."

"I could have you killed," he said.

"No, you couldn't," I said.

"Well, regardless, my offer to you stands. I like how you work."

"You're a criminal, Lyle," I said. "And by tomorrow at this time, I can promise you that your world will be crashing down around you."

"I'm Teflon, like Gotti."

"Gotti's dead," Sam said, which caused Lyle to take

a step back from us. "And just like you, he was surrounded by guys who snitched him out."

"Who are you?" Lyle said to me. He wasn't angry. He wasn't even sad, though he should have been, since news reports said at least twenty-five men were dead between the two gangs. He actually sounded genuinely curious. Maybe he just wanted to know who was going to be behind his eventual perp walk.

"My name is Michael Westen," I said. "I'm a spy."

burn notice

A USA ORIGINAL SERIES
THURSDAYS

characters welcome.

USA

BURN NOTICE: THE FIX

by

TOD GOLDBERG

First in the series based on the critically
acclaimed USA Network television show!

Covert spy Michael Westen has found himself in
forced seclusion in Miami—and a little paranoid.
Watched by the FBI, cut off from intelligence
contacts, and with his assets frozen, Westen is on ice
with a warning: stay there or get "disappeared."

And don't miss
Burn Notice: The End Game

**Available wherever books are sold or at
penguin.com**